CASSANDRA

CHRISTA WOLF

Translated from the German by
JAN VAN HEURCK

DAUNT BOOKS

This edition first published in Great Britain in 2013
by Daunt Books
83 Marylebone High Street
London W1U 4QW

1

Copyright © Christa Wolf 1983
Translation © Farrar, Straus and Giroux 1984

First published in Great Britain in 1984
by Virago Press Ltd.
Originally published in Germany in 1983 by
Hermann Luchterhand Verlag GmbH & Co KG,
Darmstadt und Neuwied.

The right of Christa Wolf to be identified as the author
of the Work has been asserted by her in accordance
with the Copyright, Designs and Patents Act 1988.

A CIP catalogue record for this title is
available from the British Library.

ISBN 978 1 907970 11 5

Typeset by Antony Gray
Printed and bound by
T J International Ltd, Padstow, Cornwall

www.dauntbooks.co.uk

TRANSLATOR'S NOTE

In 1980 East German author Christa Wolf took a trip
to Greece accompanied by her husband, Gerhard. In
1982 she was awarded a guest lectureship at the
University of Frankfurt, where in May she delivered a
series of five 'Lectures on Poetics' relating to her
Greek travels and studies. The fifth 'lecture' was a
draft of the novel *Cassandra*, which she then revised
and expanded for publication. The four introductory
lectures were published separately in Germany under
the title *Conditions of a Narrative: Cassandra; The
Frankfurt Lectures on Poetics (Voraussetzungen einer
Erzählung: Kassandra). Conditions of a Narrative:
Cassandra* is included in the ebook edition of
Cassandra, also published by Daunt Books.

Once again limb-loosing love shakes me,
bitter-sweet, untamable, a dusky animal.

SAPPHO

IT WAS HERE. This is where she stood. These stone lions looked at her; now they no longer have heads. This fortress – once impregnable, now a pile of stones – was the last thing she saw. A long-forgotten enemy demolished it, so did the centuries, sun, rain, wind. The sky is still the same, a deep blue block, high, vast. Nearby, the giant fitted-stone walls which, today as in the past, point the way to the gate, where no trace of blood can be seen seeping out from beneath. Point the way into the darkness. Into the slaughterhouse. And alone.

Keeping step with the story, I make my way into death.

Here I end my days, helpless, and nothing, nothing I could have done or not done, willed or thought, could have led me to a different goal. Deeper than any other feeling, deeper even than my fear, this imbues, etches, poisons me: the indifference of the celestials to us of earth. Unavailing the venture to set our little warmth against their icy chill. Vain our attempt to evade their atrocities, long have I known that. But a couple of nights ago on the sea crossing, when storms threatened to smash our ship from every direction; when no one could hold on unless he was lashed down; when I found Marpessa secretly untying the knots which bound her and the twins to each other and to the mast, and being attached to a longer rope than the others, I threw myself at her unhesitatingly and unthinkingly to prevent her from abandoning the lives of her children and mine to the indifferent elements, so that I could surrender them to mad people instead; when, shrinking from her gaze, I crouched again in my place beside the whimpering, spewing Agamemnon – I could only marvel at the durable stuff of those cords that bind us to life. I saw that Marpessa, who, as once in the past, would not talk to me, was better prepared for what we are suffering now than I, the seeress; for I derived joy from everything I saw – joy, not hope! – and lived on in order to see.

Strange how every person's weapons – Marpessa's silence, Agamemnon's blustering – must always remain unchanged. I, to be sure, have gradually put down my weapons; that was what proved possible for me in the way of change.

Why did I want the gift of prophecy, come what may?

To speak with my voice: the ultimate. I did not want anything more, anything different. If need be, I could prove that, but to whom? To the foreigners, impudent and reserved at the same time, who are standing around the chariot? Enough to make you laugh if anything still can: that my proneness to justify myself should have gone down only just before I did.

Marpessa does not speak. I will not see the children again. She is hiding them from me underneath her shawl.

The same sky over Mycenae as over Troy, only empty. Shiny like enamel, inaccessible, polished clean. Something in me matches the emptiness of the sky above the enemy land. So far, everything that has befallen me has struck an answering chord. This is the secret that encircles and holds me together; I have never been able to talk of it with anyone. Only here, at the uttermost rim of my life, can I name it to myself: there is something of everyone in me, so I have belonged completely to no one, and I have even understood their hatred for me. Once 'in the past' – yes, that's the magic word – I tried to talk about it to Myrine, in hints and broken phrases. Not to obtain relief, there was no relief; but because I believed I owed it to her. Troy's end was in sight, we were lost. Aeneas had pulled out with his people. Myrine despised him. And I tried to tell her – no, not just that I understood Aeneas; that I *knew* him. As if I were he. As if I were crouching inside him, feeding in thought on his traitorous resolves. 'Traitorous,' said Myrine, angrily raining axe blows on the undergrowth in the trench surrounding the citadel, not listening to me, perhaps not even understanding what I said, for since I was imprisoned in the basket I speak softly. It is not my voice that suffered, as they all thought. It is the tone. The tone of annunciation is gone. Happily gone.

Myrine shrieked. Strange that I, who am not yet old myself, must speak of almost everyone I knew in the past tense. Not of Aeneas, no. Aeneas is alive. But must a man who lives when all men die be a coward? Was it more than policy that moved him to retreat with the last men to Mount Ida, his native territory, rather than lead them to death? After all, a few of us must survive (Myrine denied that): who better than Aeneas and his people?

Why not me, along with him? The question was not asked. He, who tried to ask it, ended by taking it back. Just as I, alas, had to suppress what I could have said to him only now. In turn, I stayed alive long enough at least to think it. Will stay alive, for another few hours. I will not ask for the dagger which I know Marpessa is carrying on her. Which her eyes alone offered me a short time ago when we saw the wife, the queen. Which my eyes alone declined. Who knows me better than Marpessa? No one any more. It is past noon. What I grasp between now and evening will perish with me. Will it perish? Once a thought comes into the world, does it live on in someone else? Inside our trusty chariot driver, who finds us a nuisance?

'She's laughing,' I hear the women say; they do not know that I speak their language. They draw from me shuddering; everywhere I get the same reaction. Myrine, seeing me smile as I talked of Aeneas, shrieked: unteachable, that's what I was. I laid my hand on the nape of her neck until she was still, and from the wall beside the Scaean Gate both of us watched the sun sink into the sea. We knew it was the last time we would stand together this way.

I am testing for pain. I am probing my memory the way a doctor probes a limb to see whether it has atrophied. Perhaps pain dies before we die. That information, if true, must be passed on; but to whom? Of those here who speak my language, there is none who will not die with me. I make the pain test and think about the goodbyes. Each one was different. In the end we identified each other by whether or not we knew this was goodbye. Sometimes we just raised our hands lightly. Sometimes we embraced. Aeneas and I did not touch each other any more. It seems to me that his eyes, whose colour I could not fathom, were above me for an infinite time. Sometimes we continued to talk, the way I talked with Myrine, so that at last the name was named which we had kept silent so long: Penthesilea.

I talked of how I had seen her, Myrine, march through this gate three or four years before beside Penthesilea and her armoured band. Of my rush of irreconcilable feelings – amazement, compassion, admiration, horror, embarrassment, and yes, even an infamous amusement: how they found release in a laughing fit which distressed me and which Penthesilea was never able to pardon me for, hyper-sensitive as she was. Myrine confirmed the fact. Penthesilea was offended. This and nothing else was the reason for her coldness toward me. And I confessed to Myrine that my bids for reconciliation were half-hearted, even though I knew that Penthesilea was going to fall in battle. 'How could you know that!' Myrine asked me with a trace of her former violence; but I was no longer jealous of Penthesilea. The dead are not jealous of each other. 'She fell in battle because she wanted to fall. Why else do you think she came to Troy? And I had reason to keep close watch on her, so I saw how it was.' Myrine was silent. What had always enchanted me more than anything else about her was her hatred for my prophecies, which I never uttered in her presence, to be sure; but they were always reported to her promptly, including the passing mention of my certainty that I was going to be killed. She would not let me get away with that, unlike the others. Where did I get the right to make such pronouncements? I did not answer, closed my eyes in happiness. At last, after such a long time, my body again. Once again the hot stab through my insides. Once again the utter weakness for someone. How she tore into me. So I had not cared for Penthesilea, the man-killing warrior woman, eh? She asked. Well, did I think that she, Myrine, had killed fewer men than her commander in chief? When in fact she had most likely killed more, after Penthesilea's death, in order to avenge her?

Yes, my pony, but that was something else again.

That was your clenched defiance and your blazing grief for Penthesilea, don't you think I understood that? Then there was her deep shrinking shyness, her fear of being touched, which I never infringed until the moment when I was allowed to wind her blonde mane around my hand and so found out how very much I had felt like doing that for so long. Your smile in the moment of my death, I thought; and because I no longer abstained from any caress, I left the terror behind for a long time. Now it approaches me darkly once again.

Myrine got into my blood the moment I saw her, bright, daring, ardent beside the dark, self-consuming Penthesilea. Joy-giver or pain-giver, I could not let her go; but I do not wish she was beside me now. I rejoiced to see her, a woman, put on her weapons – she was the only one to do so – when the men of Troy brought the Greeks' horse into the city against my objections. I strengthened her resolve to keep watch beside the monster while I stayed with her, unarmed. I rejoiced, perversely again, to see her hurl herself at the first Greek to come up out of the wooden steed around midnight. Rejoiced – yes, rejoiced! – to see her fall and die from a single blow. Because I was laughing they spared me as the lives of madmen are spared.

I had not yet seen enough.

I do not want to speak any more. All the vanities and habits have been gutted; the places inside me where they could have grown back are laid waste. I feel no more sorry for myself than for others. I no longer want to prove anything. The laughter of this queen when Agamemnon stepped onto the red carpet went beyond all proof.

Who will find a voice again, and when?

It will be one whose skull is split by a pain. And until then, until his coming, nothing will be heard but bellows and commands and whimpers and the 'yes, sirs' of those who obey. The helplessness of the victors who silently prowl around the vehicle, passing each other my name. Old men, women, children. Their helplessness at the atrocity of the victory. At its aftermath, which I can already see in their blind eyes. Stricken blind indeed. Everything they have to know will unfold right before their eyes, and they will see nothing. That is just how it is.

Now I can put to use a skill I have practised all my life: to conquer my feelings by thought. In the past it was love I had to conquer; now fear. It assailed me when the chariot, dragged slowly up the mountain by weary horses, came to a stop between the sombre walls. Outside this final gate. When the sky opened and sunlight fell on the stone lions, which looked away past me and everything, and always will look away. Of course I know what fear is, but this is something different. Perhaps it is cropping up in me for the first time only to be killed again at once. Now the inner core is being razed.

My curiosity – about myself as well as about others – is fully at liberty now. When I recognised this I shrieked out loud. It was during the crossing; I was wretched like all the others, buffeted by the heavy sea, drenched to the skin by the spurting foam, disturbed by the wailing and exhalations of the other Trojan women, who were not kindly disposed toward me: for everyone always knew who I was. I was never permitted to lose myself in their midst. I wished for that too late; I did too much in my past life to make myself known. Self-reproaches, too, prevent the important questions from coming together. Now the question grew like fruit inside the peel, and when it detached itself and lay before me, I shrieked aloud, with pain or bliss.

Why did I want the gift of prophecy, come what may?

As it happened, on that stormy night King Aga-memnon the 'Most Resolute' (ye gods!) grabbed me out of the tangle of other bodies; my cry coincided with this moment and required no further explanation. I, I was the one who had stirred up Poseidon against him, he shrieked at me, out of his head with fear; for had he not sacrificed three of his best horses to the god before the crossing? 'And Athena?' I asked coldly. 'What did you sacrifice to her?' I saw him turn pale.

All men are self-centred children. (What about Aeneas? Nonsense. Aeneas is an adult.) What, mockery, in the eyes of a woman? They cannot stand that. The victorious king would have killed me – that is what I wanted him to do – if he had not still been afraid of me as well. The man has always taken me for a witch. He wanted me to pacify Poseidon! He thrust me to the bow, jerked my arms up in the posture he considered suitable for an incantation. I moved my lips. You poor wretch, what does it matter to you whether you drown here or are murdered at home?

If Clytemnestra was the woman I thought she was, she could not share the throne with this nonentity. She *is* the woman I thought she was. Besides that, she is racked with hatred. Most likely the weakling treated her vilely while he still controlled her, the way they all do. I not only know men but women as well, which is more difficult; and so I know that the queen cannot spare my life. A short time ago her glances told me so.

When did my hatred disappear? Oh yes, it is gone, my plump juicy hate. I know one name that could awaken it, but I prefer to leave that name unthought as yet. If only I could. If only I could wipe out the name, not merely from my memory, but from the memory of all men living. If I could burn it out of our heads – I would not have lived in vain. Achilles.

If only my mother had not come to mind just now, Hecuba, aboard another ship headed toward other shores with Odysseus. Who can help the thoughts that come into his head? Her crazed face as they dragged her away. Her mouth. My mother called down on the Greeks the most hideous curse ever uttered in human history. It will come true, one must only know how to wait. I called out to her that her curse would be fulfilled. Her last word was my name, a scream of triumph. When I stepped into the ship, everything in me was dumb.

That night the storm abated soon after I 'charmed' it. Not only my fellow captives, but also the Greeks – even the crude, avid oarsmen – drew back from me, shy and deferential. I told Agamemnon I would lose my power if he forced me into his bed. He let me go. His potency was already long gone; the girl who lived with him in his tent for the last year betrayed it to me. He had threatened that if she did this – betrayed his unutterable secret – he would find a pretext to have her stoned to death by his troops. Suddenly I understood his exquisite cruelty in battle, just as I understood why his silence deepened the farther we got from Nauplion along the long, dusty road through the plains of Argos, and the closer we came to his citadel: Mycenae. The closer we came to his wife, to whom he had never given a reason to be merciful if he showed any weakness. Who knows what misery she may spare him if she murders him.

They do not know how to live; this is the real disaster, the truly fatal danger – I came to understand that only little by little. I, the seeress! Priam's daughter. How long I was blind to the obvious: that I had to choose between my birth and my office. How long I feared the dread I must arouse in my people if I were to perform that office, come what may. The same dread that has now hurried ahead of me over the sea. The people here – naïve if I compare them with the Trojans, for they have not experienced war – are exhibiting their feelings, fingering the chariot, the foreign objects, the plundered weapons, even the horses. Not me. The chariot driver, who seems ashamed of his countrymen, told them my name. I saw the same thing I am used to seeing: their dread. 'They are not the best people, of course,' says the chariot driver. 'They stayed at home.' The women approach again. They appraise me unabashed, peer under the shawl I have drawn over my head and shoulders. They bicker about whether I am beautiful; the older ones claim I am, the younger say no.

Beautiful? I, the terrible one. I who wanted Troy to fall.

Rumour, which overruns the seas, will also precede me into time. Panthous the Greek will turn out to be right. 'But you are lying, my dear,' he said to me while we performed the prescribed passes at the shrine of Apollo, readying the ceremony. 'You are lying when you prophesy we are all doomed. Prophesying our destruction, you immortalise your-self. You need that more than you need a snug life in the present. Your name will go on. And you know it.'

I could not slap his face yet a second time. Panthous was jealous, spiteful, and sharp-tongued. But was he right? In any case, he made me think the unheard-of: the world could go on after our destruction. I did not let him see how that unnerved me. Why had I allowed myself to suppose that the human race would be wiped out along with us? Did I not know how the female slaves from the conquered tribe were always forced to increase the fertility of the victors? Was it the overweening pride of a king's daughter that made me implicate all the Trojan women – not to mention the men – in the death of our house? It took me a long time and much labour to distinguish between qualities in ourselves that we know and those that are inborn and virtually unrecognisable. Affable, modest, unassuming – that was the image I had of myself, which survived every catastrophe virtually intact. Not only that: whenever it survived, the catastrophe lay behind me. Did I gravely wound the self-esteem of my family in order to preserve my own – because to be honest, proud, and truth-loving was a part of this image? Did I pay them back for injuries they had inflicted on me by the inflexible way I spoke the truth? I believe that this is what Panthous the Greek thought about me. It took me a long time to notice, but he knew and detested himself, and sought relief by attributing one cause and one alone to every act or omission: self-love. He was absolutely convinced of a world order in which it was impossible to serve one-self and others at the same time. Never, never was there a breach in his aloneness. But he had no right – I know that today – to regard me as like himself. At first perhaps he was right to think me like him, on one score – what Marpessa called my pride. I lived on to experience the happiness of becoming myself and being more useful to others because of it. I do know that only a few people notice when someone changes. Hecuba, my mother, knew me when I was young and ceased to concern herself with me. 'This child does not need me,' she said. I admired and hated her for it. Priam, my father, needed me.

When I turn around I see Marpessa smiling. Now that things have taken a grave turn, I hardly see her without a smile. 'Marpessa, the children will not be allowed to live; they're mine. You will, I think.' 'I know,' she says. She does not say whether she wants to live or not. They will have to drag the children away from her. Perhaps they will have to break her arms. Not because they are mine, but because they are children. 'I'll be the first to go, Marpessa. Right after the king.' Marpessa answers: 'I know.' 'Your pride, Marpessa, overshadows even mine.' And she, smiling, replies: 'That's how it must be, mistress.'

How many years it has been since she called me mistress. Where she led me I was not mistress, not priestess. That I was allowed that experience makes dying easier for me. Easier? Do I know what I am saying?

I will never know whether this woman whose love I courted loved me. At first it may be that I did it from coquetry: in the past something in me wanted to please. Later I did it because I wanted to know her. She served me to the point of self-abandon, and so she must have needed to exercise reserve.

When the fear ebbs away, as it is doing just now, remote thoughts come to mind. Why did the prisoners from Mycenae describe their Lion Gate as even more gigantic than it looks to me? Why did they portray the cyclopean walls as more immense than they are, their people as more violent and avid for vengeance? They talked gladly and extravagantly about their home, like all captives. Not one ever asked me why I was gathering such exact intelligence about the enemy land. And why, in fact, did I do so, at a time when even to me it seemed certain that we were winning? We were supposed to smite the enemy, not to know him! What impelled me to know him, when I could reveal to no one my shocking discovery: they are like us!? Was I trying to find out where I was going to die? Was I thinking about dying? Wasn't I swollen with triumph like all of us?

How quickly and completely we forget.

War gives its people their shape. I do not want to remember them that way, as they were made and shattered by war. I gave a crack on the mouth to that minstrel who went on singing the glory of Priam until the end: the undignified, flattering wretch. No. I will not forget my confused, wayward father. But neither will I forget the father I loved more than anyone else when I was a child. Who was not too particular about reality. Who could live in fantasy worlds. Who did not have clearly in view the contingencies that maintained his nation, or those that threatened him. This made him less than the ideal king, but he was the husband of the ideal queen; that gave him special privileges. I can still see him: night after night he used to go in to my often-pregnant mother, who sat in her megaron, in her wooden armchair, which closely resembled a throne, where the king, smiling amiably, drew up a stool. This is the earliest picture I remember, for I, Father's favourite and interested in politics like none of my numerous siblings, was allowed to sit with them and listen to what they were saying; often seated in Priam's lap, my hand in the crook of his shoulder (the place I love best on Aeneas), which was very vulnerable and where I myself saw the Greek spear run him through. It was I, who forever afterward confused with the ascetic, clean odour of my father the names of foreign princes, kings, and cities; the goods we traded or transported through the Hellespont on our famous ships; the figures of our income and the debates about their expenditure. (Now those princes are fallen, the cities impoverished or destroyed, the goods spoiled or plundered.) It was I, I of all his children my father believed, who betrayed our city and betrayed him.

Nothing left to describe the world but the language of the past. The language of the present has shrivelled to the words that describe this dismal fortress. The language of the future has only one sentence left for me: Today I will be killed.

What does the man want? Is he speaking to me? 'I must be hungry,' he says. Not I, he is the one who is hungry; he wants to stable the horses and go home at last, to his family, who surround him impatiently. I am to follow his queen, he says. Quietly enter the fortress with the two guards, who are attending me for my protection, not to keep watch on me. I will have to terrify him. 'Yes,' I say to him, 'I am going. Only not now, not yet. Leave me here a little while yet. The reason is, you know,' (I say to him, trying to spare him) 'When I enter this gate I am as good as dead.'

The same old story: not the crime but its heralding turns men pale and furious. I know that from my own example. Know that we would rather punish the one who names the deed than the one who commits it. In this respect, as in everything else, we are all alike. The difference lies in whether we know it.

It was hard for me to learn that, because I was accustomed to being the exception and did not want to be lumped under the same roof with everyone else. That is why I struck Panthous on the evening of the day he consecrated me as a priestess; when he said to me: 'Tough luck for you, little Cassandra, that you are your father's favourite daughter. You know that Polyxena would make a more suitable priestess. She prepared herself, whereas you are relying on his support. And, it seems' – I thought his smile impudent when he said that – 'you are also relying on your dreams.'

I slapped his face for that. He gave me a penetrating look, but all he said was: 'And now you are relying on the fact that although I am the chief priest, I am, after all, only a Greek.'

What he said was true, but not completely, for less than he could imagine was I guided by self-interest. (Yes, I know, unbeknown to us even our self-interest is guided by something!) The dream of the night before came unsummoned, and it troubled me deeply. It was Apollo who came to me, I saw that at once despite his distant resemblance to Panthous; although I could hardly have said wherein the resemblance consisted. Most likely in the expression of his eyes, which I called 'cruel' then but merely 'clear-headed' later on; referring to Panthous, for I never saw Apollo again! I saw Apollo bathed in radiant light the way Panthous taught me to see him. The sun god with his lyre, his blue although cruel eyes, his bronzed skin. Apollo, the god of the seers. Who knew what I ardently desired: the gift of prophecy, and conferred it on me with a casual gesture which I did not dare to feel was disappointing; whereupon he approached me as a man. I believed it was only due to my awful terror that he transformed himself into a wolf surrounded by mice and spat furiously into my mouth when he was unable to overpower me. So that when I awoke in horror I had an unspeakably loathsome taste on my tongue, and in the middle of the night I fled out of the temple precinct, where I was required to sleep at that time, into the citadel, into the palace, into the room, into my mother's bed. For me it was a precious moment when Hecuba's face twisted with concern for me; but she had herself under control. 'A wolf?' she asked coolly. 'Why a wolf? How did you come to think of that? And where did you get the mice from? Who told you that?'

Apollo Lykeios. The voice of Parthena, the wet-nurse. The god of the wolves and the mice: she knew dark stories about him which she whispered to me and which I was not supposed to repeat to anyone. I would never have thought that this ambivalent god could be identical to our unimpeachable Apollo in the temple. Only Marpessa, Parthena's daughter and the same age I was, knew about the stories and kept silent as I did. My mother did not insist that I name names, for she was less troubled by the wolf shape of the sun god than by my fear to unite with him.

It was an honour for a mortal woman if a god wanted to lie with her, was it not? Yes, it was. And the fact that the god I had appointed myself to serve wanted to possess me completely: wasn't that natural?

Yes of course. So, what was wrong? I should never, never have told Hecuba this dream! She would not leave off asking me prying questions.

Had I not sat one year before with the other girls in the temple grounds of Athena just after I bled for the first time – hadn't I been forced to sit there? I thought as I had thought at the time, and the skin of my scalp crawled with dreadful shame just as it had done a year before – and hadn't everything followed its pre-determined course? Even now I could point out the cypress tree under which I sat, provided that the Greeks have not set fire to it; I could describe the shape of the loose row of clouds from the Hellespont. 'Loose row.' Absurd, ridiculous words: I cannot waste any more time on them. I will simply think of the scent of olives and tamarisks. Close my eyes, I can't go on; but I could. I opened them a crack and let in the legs of men. Dozens of men's legs clad in sandals; you would not believe how different they all were, and all repulsive. In a single day I had enough of men's legs to last me a lifetime; no one suspected. I felt their looks on my face, on my breast. Not once did I look around at the other girls, they did not look at me. We had nothing to do with each other; it was up to the men to select and deflower us. For a long time before I went to sleep I heard the snapping of fingers and the single phrase uttered with so many different intonations: 'Come on.' All around me the emptiness grew. One by one the other girls had been taken away: the daughters of the officers, the palace scribes, the potters, the craftsmen, the charioteers, and the tenant farmers. I had known emptiness since my earliest childhood. I experienced two kinds of shame: that of being elect and that of being left on the shelf. Yes, I would become a priestess at any cost.

At noon, when Aeneas came, it struck me that for a long time now I had picked out his figure from every crowd. He came straight over to me. 'Forgive me,' he said, 'I could not come before now.' As if we had had an appointment. He lifted me up – no, I got up myself; but we disagreed about that now and again. We went into a remote corner of the temple precinct and, without noticing it, crossed over the boundary beyond which one may not speak. It was not due to pride that I never said a word to the women about Aeneas when we gradually came to speak about our feelings; and not only due to shyness, although of course that played a part. I always held back; I never showed my inner self as other women did. I know that because of this I never broke down the barrier between us completely. The unspoken name of Aeneas stood between me and the women, who as the war dragged on came to fear their increasingly savage menfolk as much as the enemy, and who could not know whose side I was really on if I would tell them no details: no details, for example, about that afternoon at the boundary of the temple precinct when we two, Aeneas and I, both knew what was expected of us; for we had both been instructed by my mother, Hecuba. That afternoon, when neither of us felt capable of living up to these expectations. When each of us felt to blame for our failure. My nurse and my mother and Herophile the priestess had impressed on me the duties of consummation, but they had not reckoned on the fact that the sudden intervention of love can obstruct these duties; so not knowing which way to turn, I burst into tears at his uncertainty, even though his uncertainty could only be due to my awkwardness. We were young, young. As he kissed, stroked, and touched me, I would have done whatever he wanted; but he seemed to want nothing. He asked me to forgive him for something, but I did not understand what. Toward evening I fell asleep. I still remember dreaming about a ship that carried Aeneas away from our coast across calm blue water, and about a huge fire which interposed itself between the voyagers and us, who stayed behind, as the ship moved away toward the horizon. The sea was burning. I can still see this dream-image today, no matter how many grimmer pictures of reality have veiled it since. I would like to know – what am I thinking! Like to know? I? But yes, the words are true – I would like to know what unrest, unremarked by me, already caused such dreams amid peace, amid happiness: for believe it or not, we used to talk of happiness and peace!

I woke up screaming. Aeneas, stirred awake, could

not quiet me and carried me to my mother. Not until later, not until I felt compelled to examine these events day and night until they gradually lost their keen edge, did I wonder at how my mother asked him whether everything had gone all right, and how he, Aeneas, curtly answered 'Yes.' And how Hecuba thereupon thanked him. That was the strangest part of all, and humiliating, although I did not know why. And she sent him away. Put me to bed like a child after administering a potion which made me feel good and dissolved all questions and all dreams.

It is hard to put into words what signs tell us infallibly when we must not reflect further about an event. Aeneas vanished from my view, the first instance of what became a pattern. Aeneas remained a glowing point inside me; his name a sharp stab that I inflicted on myself as often as I could. But I would not allow myself to understand the enigmatic sentence of Parthena, my nurse, when she took leave of me – for now I was an adult – and gave me her daughter Marpessa as a maidservant. In a tone half respectful, half hate-filled, she murmured to herself: 'So the old lady has gotten her way again even if this time, maybe, it's for her little daughter's good.' And then she, too, asked me if everything had gone all right. And I told her my dream as I had always done. For the first time I saw a human being turn pale at my words. (What did that really feel like? Frightening? Exciting? Did it give me an appetite for more? Later on, they accused me of needing to see people turn pale. Is that true?)

'Cybele, help!' whispered Parthena, my nurse. These were the same words she spoke when she died – shortly after the destruction of Troy and before the sea crossing, I believe. Yes, when all we captives were rounded up on the naked shore in the terrible storms of autumn, the quaking storms at the end of the world. 'Cybele, help!' moaned the old woman. But it was her daughter Marpessa who helped her, giving her a potion which put Parthena to sleep, never more to awaken.

Who was Cybele?

The nurse recoiled. I could see that she was forbidden to speak that name. She knew, and I knew too, that Hecuba must be obeyed. Today it seems to me incredible how her orders affected me; I can hardly remember that I once rebelled against them in high dudgeon. All she had ever wanted was to protect me, she told me afterward. But she had underestimated me, she said. By that time I had seen Cybele.

No matter how often I walked that way in later years, alone and with the other women, I have never forgotten how I felt when Marpessa led me to Mount Ida one evening at twilight – I had always had the mountain in full view, secretly loved it as my own, walked there countless times, thought I knew it – and how Marpessa, leading the way, dived into a shrub-covered fold in the ground. How she crossed through a small grove of fig trees on paths where only goats clambered, and how we suddenly stood surrounded by young oak trees, before the sanctuary of the unknown goddess where a band of brown-skinned, slender-limbed women danced in homage. Among them I saw slave women from the palace, women from the settlements beyond the walls of the citadel, and also Parthena the nurse, who crouched outside the cave entrance, under the willow tree whose roots dangled into the opening of the cave like the pubic hair of a woman: she seemed to be directing the train of dancers with movements of her massive body. Marpessa slid into the circle, which did not even notice my arrival – a new and actually painful experience for me. They gradually increased their tempo, intensified their rhythm, moved faster, more demandingly, more turbulently; hurled individual dancers out of the circle, among them Marpessa, my reserved Marpessa!; drove them to gestures which offended my modesty; until, beside themselves, they shook, went into howling contortions, sank into an ecstasy in which they saw things invisible to the rest of us, and finally one after another sagged and collapsed in exhaustion. Marpessa was one of the last.

I fled in awe and terror, wandered around for a long time, came home late at night, found my bed ready, a meal prepared, Marpessa waiting beside the bed. And next morning in the palace, the same unruffled faces as always.

What was happening? What kind of place did I live in? How many realities were there in Troy besides mine, which I had thought was the only one? Who fixed the boundary between visible and invisible? And who allowed the ground to be shaken where I had walked so securely? 'I know who Cybele is!' I shrieked at my mother. 'So,' said Hecuba. 'That's fine, then.' No questions about who had taken me there. No investigation. No punishment. Did my mother show a trace of relief, even weakness? What was that to me, a mother who showed weakness? Did she perhaps intend to confide her worries to me? Then I withdrew. Evaded the touch of real people as I would do for a long time to come. Needed and demanded to be unapproachable. Became a priestess. Yes. She got to know me sooner than I did her, after all.

'The queen,' my father said to me in one of our intimate hours, 'Hecuba dominates only those who can be dominated. She loves the indomitable ones.' All at once I saw my father in a different light. Surely Hecuba must love him? No doubt of it. Did that mean he was indomitable? Ah. Once upon a time our parents were young, too. As the war went on, baring everyone's entrails, the picture changed. Priam became increasingly unapproachable and obstinate, yet controllable all the same; only it was no longer Hecuba who could control him. Hecuba grew softer, yet could not be swayed. Grief for his sons killed Priam before he was pierced by the enemy spear.

Hecuba, forced open by pain, grew more compassion-
ate and more alive with each year of woe.

Like me. Never was I more alive than now, in the
hour of my death.

What do I mean by alive? What I mean by alive – not
to shrink from what is most difficult: to change one's
image of oneself. 'Words,' said Panthous in the days
when he was still my fencing partner. 'Nothing but
words, Cassandra. A human being changes nothing,
so why himself of all things, why of all things his
image of himself?'

If I grope my way back along the thread of my life,
which is rolled up inside me – I skip over the war, a
black block; slowly, longingly backtrack to the pre-
war years; the time as a priestess, a white block;
farther back: the girl – here I am caught by the very
word 'girl,' and caught all the more by her form. By
the beautiful image. I have always been caught by
images more than by words. Probably that is strange,
and incompatible with my vocation; but I can no
longer pursue my vocation. The last thing in my life
will be a picture, not a word. Words die before
pictures.

Mortal fear.

What will it be like? Will I be overcome by weakness?
Will my body take control of my thinking? Will the
mortal fear simply reoccupy, with a powerful thrust,
all the positions I have wrested from my ignorance, my
comfortableness, my pride, my cowardice, laziness,

shame? Will it successfully sweep away even the resolution I sought and formulated on the way here: that I will not lose consciousness until the end?

When our ships – how stupid! I mean *their* ships – moored in the bay of Nauplion during a calm while the water was smooth as glass and the sun, plump and gorged with blood, was sinking behind the chain of mountains; when my Trojan women sought consolation in inconsolable weeping, as if they had become truly captives only now, when they set foot in the foreign land; in the days following, on the dusty, hot, arduous path through the stronghold of Tiryns and the filthy market towns of Argos, met and accompanied by the abuse of the women and old men who gathered; but especially on the last stretch climbing up through dry land toward this terrible stone pile, the fortress of Mycenae, our destination, which loomed overhead, sinister but still remote; when even Marpessa moaned aloud; when the king himself, irresolute Agamemnon, instead of urging haste as one would have expected, ordered one rest stop after another and each time sat down silently beside me in the shade of an olive (olive, tenderest tree . . .), where he drank and offered me wine in a way that offended no one in his retinue; when my heart, which I had stopped feeling long ago, grew smaller, firmer, harder with each rest stop, a smarting stone from which I could not wring another drop of moisture: *then* my resolution was formed, smelted, tempered, forged, and cast like a spear. I will continue a witness even if there is no longer one single human being left to demand my testimony.

I did not want to give myself the chance to ponder this resolution again. But isn't it the kind of remedy that causes a worse ill than it is meant to combat? Has not this tried and tested remedy already brought about a renewal of my old, forgotten malady: inner division, so that I watch myself, see myself sitting in this accursed Greek chariot trembling with fear beneath my shawl? Will I split myself in two until the end before the axe splits me, for the sake of consciousness? In order not to writhe with fear, not to bellow like an animal – and who should know better than I how animals bellow when they are sacrificed! Will I, until the end, until that axe – will I still, when my head, my neck, is already – will I—?

Why do I simply refuse to allow myself this relapse into creatureliness? What is holding me back? Who is there left to see me? Do I, the unbeliever, still see myself as the focus of a god's gazes, as I did when a child, a girl, a priestess? Will that never pass?

Wherever I look or cast my thoughts, there is no god, no judgment, only myself. Who is it that makes my self-judgment so severe, into death and beyond?

What if that, too, is prescribed? What if that, too, is worked by strings that are out of my hands, like the movements of the girl I was, ideal image, image of longing: the bright young figure in the clear landscape, gay, candid, hopeful, trusting herself and others, deserving what they conferred on her, free; oh, free? In reality: captive. Steered, guided, and driven to the goal others set. How humiliating (a word from the old days). They all knew. Panthous too. Panthous the Greek was in on the secret. He did not twitch an eyelash as he handed over the staff and the fillet to the candidate designated by Hecuba. So he did not believe that I had dreamed of Apollo? But of course he did. 'Of course, of course, little Cassandra.' The awkward thing was, he did not believe in dreams.

On the day when I announced calmly, 'Troy will fall,' he cried, 'At last!' because I did not cite a dream as proof. He shared in my knowledge, but he did not care. He, the Greek, was not anxious for Troy, only for his own life, which he felt had lasted long enough anyhow (so he said). For a long time he had been carrying around the device to end it. But he did not use it. Died in torment in order to live one day longer. Panthous. It seems we never really knew him.

Of course Parthena, my nurse, knew what was going on behind the scenes, too. Knew how I was chosen priestess. Marpessa knew it through her. But it was she (how long it has been since I thought of that) who handed me the key to my dream and my life. 'If Apollo spits into your mouth,' she told me solemnly, 'that means you have the gift to predict the future. But no one will believe you.'

The gift of prophecy. So that was it. A hot terror. I

had dreamed of it. Believe me, not believe me – they would see. After all, in the long run it was impossible for people not to believe a person who proves she is right.

I had even won over Hecuba, my sceptical mother. Now she recalled a story about my early childhood; Parthena, my nurse, was made to spread it around; by no means were dreams our only clue. On our second birthday my twin brother, Helenus, and I fell asleep in the sacred grove of the Thymbraian Apollo, left alone by our parents, poorly tended by our nurse, who had fallen asleep, no doubt a little dazed from the heavy sweet wine. When Hecuba came to look for us, she saw to her horror that the sacred serpents of the temple had approached us and were licking at our ears. She drove away the serpents with vigorous handclapping, at the same time waking the nurse and the children. But ever since then she had known: the god had given these two children of hers the gift of prophecy. 'Is it really true?' people asked, and the more often Parthena the nurse told the story, the more firmly she believed it. I still remember that Hecuba's zeal left a flat taste in my mouth; I felt that she was going a little too far. But all the same she confirmed what I dearly wanted to believe: I, Cassandra, and none other of the twelve daughters of Priam and Hecuba, had been appointed prophetess by the god himself. What was more natural than that I should also serve him as a priestess at his shrine?

Polyxena . . . I built my career at your expense; you were no worse than I, no less suited to the post. I wanted to tell you that before they dragged you away to be a sacrificial victim, as they are doing to me now. Polyxena, even if we had exchanged lives, our deaths would have been the same. Is that a consolation? Did you need consolation? Do I need it? You looked at me (did you still see me?). I said nothing. They dragged you away, to the grave of depraved Achilles. Achilles the brute.

Oh, if only these humans did not know love.

Oh, if only I had strangled him with my own hands on that first day of the war – may his name be accursed and forgotten – instead of looking on while he, Achilles, strangled my brother Troilus. Remorse eats away at me, it will not ease, Polyxena. Panthous the Greek held me back. 'They're too much for you,' he said. 'I know them.' He knew them. And me. I would not strangle any man. Polyxena, let me enjoy my belated confessions – I fell to him, had already fallen to him when it was not yet decided which of us he would dedicate priestess: you or me. Never, my dear one, did we speak of it. Everything was said in glances, half-spoken phrases. How could I have said to you what I was scarcely able to think: 'Let me have the office of priestess; you do not need it.' That is what I thought, I swear to you. I did not see that you needed it just as I did, only for the opposite reason. You had your lovers, that is what I thought.

I was alone. After all, I used to run into them at daybreak coming out of your bedchamber. After all, I could not help seeing how beautiful you were, how you were growing more beautiful, you with your curly dark-blonde hair – the only one of Hecuba's daughters whose hair was not black. Whoever could have been your father? wondered the nurses and the palace servants. No – you had no hope of becoming Priam's favourite daughter. You did not envy me that post; that infuriated me. I was not in a position to wonder why you wanted to be priestess. To wonder whether you might not possibly want something quite different from the office than I did. Not dignity, distance, and a substitute for pleasures that were denied me, but rather, protection from yourself, from the multitude of your lovers, from the fate already prepared for you. You with your grey eyes. You with your narrow head, the white oval of your face, your hairline sharp as if it were cut with a knife. With that torrent of hair which every man had to dip his hands into. You with whom no man who saw you could help but fall in love. What do I mean, fall in love! Fall prey. And not only every man, many women, too. Marpessa among them I believe, when she came out of exile and never looked at a man again. Even 'fall prey' is too feeble a term for the frenzy of love, the madness, that gripped many a man, including Achilles the brute – and without your doing anything to cause it, that one must concede . . . Polyxena. Yes, it is quite possible that I was mistaken in the dark corridor at night; for if the shadow I saw creeping out your door was Aeneas's shadow, why should you, whose every action was performed openly, have sworn to me much later that Aeneas had never, never been with you? But how silly I was. How could it have been Aeneas, coming from one woman only to clutch at another's breast, and then run away!

Ah, Polyxena. The way you used to move. Brisk and impetuous, at the same time graceful. The way a priestess is not supposed to move. 'Why ever not!' said Panthous, and he flaunted his knowledge (of deeper authority than mine) of the nature of his god Apollo, whom after all he had served at the god's central shrine in Delphi on the Greek mainland. 'Why not be graceful, little Cassandra? Apollo is also the god of the Muses, is he not?' He knew how to insult me, that Greek. He managed to convey that he regarded as barbaric the crude profile which we peoples of Asia Minor gave his god.

Which did not mean that he considered me an unsuitable priestess. Beyond doubt, he said, certain of my character traits cut me out for the priesthood. Which traits? Well, my desire to exercise influence over people; how else could a woman hold a position of power? Second: my ardent desire to be on familiar terms with the deity. And of course my aversion to the approaches of mortal men.

Panthous the Greek behaved as if he was unaware

of the wound in my heart; as if he did not care that he was instilling in this heart a very subtle, very secret animosity toward him, the Chief Priest, of which I myself was scarcely conscious. After all, he was the one who taught me my Greek. And taught me the art of receiving a man, too. One night when I, the newly dedicated priestess, had to keep vigil by the god's image, he came to me. Skilfully, almost without hurting me and almost tenderly, he did what Aeneas (I thought of him) had been unwilling or unable to do. It seemed not to surprise him that I was untouched, or that I had such a great fear of physical pain. He never mentioned a word about that night to anyone, not even me. But I was at a loss as to how I could harbour hatred and gratitude toward one and the same man.

I have a pale memory of that time; I felt nothing. For a whole year Polyxena did not speak to me. Priam was preparing for war. I held aloof. I played the priestess. I thought, to be grown up consists in this game: to lose oneself. I did not permit disappointment. I did not allow myself the slightest mistake when I led the procession of maidens to the statue of the god. As I had expected, I was trained to lead the chorus; I succeeded at everything. At first I feared I would be punished when a wolf or even a troop of mice appeared to me during prayers instead of the radiant form of the god with the lyre; but soon I found that absolutely nothing happened if I abandoned myself pleasurably to my apparitions. When Panthous came to me too, I had to envision the other man, Aeneas, in order to convert my disgust to pleasure. Upheld by the respect of the Trojans, I lived in semblance more than ever. I still remember how my life drained out of me. I can't do it, I often thought as I sat on the city wall staring into space without seeing; but I could not bring myself to wonder what it was that placed me under such strain when my existence was so easy.

I saw nothing. Overtaxed by the gift of sight, I was blind. I saw only what was there, next to nothing. The course of the god's year and the demands of the palace determined my life. You could also say they weighed it down. I did not know it could be different. I lived between events which ostensibly comprised the history of the royal house. Events that aroused the craving for more and more new events, and finally for war.

I believe that was the first thing I really *saw*.

Rumours about the SECOND SHIP were slow to reach me. My heart bitter with renunciation, I had moved away from the great circle of my brothers and sisters, their friends and young slaves, who used to mock and criticise, whisper or loudly discuss, in the evening, the resolves the assembly reached during the day. I was not forbidden to continue my old indolent life on my free evenings, to sit around under the trees and shrubs in the inner courtyards of the citadel, to give myself to the familiar and well-loved sounds of water rippling through earthenware pipes, to surrender to the hour in which the sky grows yellow and the houses radiate outward the daylight they have absorbed; to let wash over me the never-changing murmur, whispers, and prattle of my brothers and sisters, of the teachers, nurses, and domestic slaves. I forbade it to myself after I became a priestess. After I was convinced that Polyxena had blackened my character to my brothers and sisters (which she did not so much as dream of doing, she told me later, and I could not help but believe her). After I was convinced that my idle brothers and sisters, some of whom liked gossip and family discord, had run me down to their hearts' content. I wanted to be privileged above them all, but I could not bear to have them envy me.

All this, the Troy of my childhood, no longer exists except inside my head. I will rebuild it there while I still have time, I will not forget a single stone, a single incidence of light, a single laugh, a single cry. It shall be kept faithfully inside me, however short the time may be. Now I have learned to see what is not, how hard the lesson was.

Helenus. Oh, Helenus, identical in appearance, different in kind. The image of me – if I had been a man. If only I were! I thought in despair when they made you the oracle – not me! not me! 'Oh, be glad, Sister. What a thankless job, to be a soothsayer.' Well (he said), he would observe Calchas's instructions to the letter. Helenus was no seer. He did not have the gift, he needed the ritual. All the thoughtlessness which may have been intended for us both had gone to him. All the melancholy to me. How I longed to be in his place. What was the priestess compared to the diviner! How greedily I watched him when he donned women's clothing to inspect the animal entrails at the altar stone. How he struggled to choke down his disgust at the smell of blood, the steaming viscera which I was quite used to because from early child-hood I had had the chore of disembowelling small animals for the kitchen. If only I were he. If only I could exchange my sex for his. If only I could deny it, conceal it. Yes, really, that is how I felt. Scarcely glancing at the intestines, liver, maw of the young bull, I watched the excited, gaping faces of the people who clustered around the sacrificial victim and the priest, waiting for his words as for food and drink. My brother churned out lame, conventional bulletins about sun and rain, good and bad harvests, the breeding of livestock and children. How differently I would have spoken! I would have laid down the law in quite a different tone; I would have liked to teach them something quite, quite different, those un-suspecting, easily satisfied people – namely . . . Namely? What would I have taught them then? Panthous, who kept an eye on me in those days, asked me the question point-blank. What else would I have talked about besides weather, the fertility of the soil, cattle pests, diseases. Did I want to tear the people out of their familiar round where they felt comfortable and looked for nothing else? To which I arrogantly replied: 'Because they don't know anything else. Because this sort of question is all they are allowed.'

'All they are allowed by whom? The gods? Circumstances? The king? And who are you to force other questions on them? Leave everything as it is, Cassandra, I'm giving you good advice.' When he did not come to me at night for a long spell, I missed him sorely. Not him, 'it.' And when he was lying on top of me – Aeneas, no one but Aeneas. Of course. The Greek noticed many things because he kept his reserve: so let him see this, too, for all I cared. But nothing in heaven or earth could have forced me to reveal my secret. My envy of Helenus ended as everything ends: when, I do not know. My zeal to impart new questions to mankind subsided, disappeared. I kept my secret. There are secrets that ravage you, others that make you stronger. This was one of the bad kind. Who knows how far it might have driven me if Aeneas had not really been there one day?

What are the Mycenaean women saying as they crowd around me? 'She's smiling,' they say. So I am smiling? Do I even know what that is any more: to smile? The last time I smiled was when Aeneas passed me headed toward Mount Ida with his handful of people, carrying his father, old Anchises, on his back.

It did not matter that he failed to recognise me when he looked for me among the crowd of women captives. I saw he was getting away, and smiled.

What does that old, emaciated woman want from me; what is she screaming? She is screaming that in time my laughter will pass. 'Yes,' I say. 'I know that. And soon.'

Now a guard intervenes to prevent the native population from holding any contact with slaves. So quick he is. That is something that always amazed me about the Greeks: they do what has to be done, quickly. And thoroughly. How long it would have taken our young palace Trojans, given to irony as they were, to understand the prohibition against associating with slaves. And to obey it! There would have been no question of obeying. Even Eumelos failed when it came to that point. 'People like us are trying to save you,' he said to me bitterly, 'and you all sneak off behind my back and slit your own throats.' In his way he was right. He wanted us to be the kind of people you need in a war. He wanted us to become like the enemy in order to defeat him. That did not suit us. We wanted to be like ourselves, inconsistent: that was the word Panthous tagged us with. Shrugged his shoulders, resigned. 'It won't work, Cassandra,' he said. 'That's not the way you wage war against the Greeks.' He must have known what he was talking about. After all, he had run away from the consistency of the Greeks, had he not? He did not talk about it.

He kept his true concerns to himself. You had to reconstruct his motives from reports, rumours, and observation.

One thing struck me early on: his fear of pain. His hypersensitivity. He never risked physical combat. But it occurs to me that I was noted for my endurance of pain. For my ability to hold my hand over the flame longer than anyone else, without grimacing, without crying. I noticed that Panthous used to walk away when I did that. I attributed it to sympathy for me. It was overstimulated nerves. Much later I realised that a person's attitude to pain reveals more about his future than almost any other sign I know. When did my own haughty attitude to pain break down? When the war started, of course. When I saw the fear of the men. For what was their fear of battle if not the fear of physical pain? The curious tricks they used to deny the fear or run away from the pain, from the battle. Yet the fear of the Greeks seemed to surpass our own by far. 'Naturally,' said Panthous. 'They are fighting on foreign soil. You are fighting at home.' So what was he doing among us, this foreigner? You could not ask him.

This much was known: Panthous was a prize that Cousin Lampos brought back on the FIRST SHIP. That is how the palace referred to the enterprise once a second and a third ship had followed the first and it was decided at last to withdraw the common folk's term, 'ship to Delphi,' from circulation and substitute neutral designations. That is how Anchises, Aeneas's father, explained it to the king's daughter, the priestess, when he taught me the history of Troy: short and to the point. 'Just you listen, girl.' (Anchises's long head. The high, completely bald skull. The multitude of wrinkles running the breadth of his forehead. The thick eyebrows. The bright crafty gaze. The mobile features. The forceful chin. The irascible mouth, often gaping or twisted with laughter, more often in a grin. The slender, powerful hands with their nails worn down by toil: Aeneas's hands.) 'So listen now. It's really very simple. Someone (your father, for all I know, although I doubt he had the idea himself, I'd bet it was Calchas) – someone, I say, sends a cousin of the royal family, this Lampos, who makes a very serviceable port administrator, but as a king's envoy on a delicate assignment? – sends Lampos with a ship on a top-secret mission to Greece. He's foolish – or let's say imprudent – enough to order the people to cheer as the ship leaves harbour.' 'Me too, Anchises,' I said. 'Held on my nurse's arm. Light, cheers, banners, sparkling water, and an enormous ship: my earliest memory.' 'We've hit on the point already. An enormous ship. Permit me to smile. A modest little ship, I would almost say: a boat. Because the thing is, if we had been in a position to furnish an enormous ship, we would not have sent it to Greece of all places. Because in that case we would not have needed these pushy Greeks, or to have paid our respects to their oracle. We would not have entered into negotiations about our hereditary right: access to the Hellespont. Well then, to sum up the result: the Greeks did not agree on terms, Lampos brought rich offerings to Delphi which we could barely afford; Panthous saw him there, became part of his retinue, came back here with him. So when the ship sailed in, there were spoils of a kind, to show the cheering crowd. And our palace scribes, who as you must know are a breed unto themselves, have belatedly rechristened this the FIRST SHIP, bragging about an enterprise that halfway miscarried.'

Oi, oi. But Anchises's stringent clear-headedness never lacked for a kind of poetry either; I could not resist that. Besides, he himself had been one of the leaders of the SECOND SHIP, and so was undeniably an authority. But altogether a different story was heard in the inner courts, where we quarrelled about nothing as heatedly as the FIRST SHIP. Hector, the eldest of my brothers, then a strongly built young man with a rather too soft disposition, categorically denied that Operation One had been successful in any way. Cousin Lampos was not sent to the Delphic oracle to haul away a priest, he said. 'No? Why was he sent then?' Hector had the story, half-officially, from the priests: Lampos was supposed to ask the Pythia whether the hill upon which Troy stood was still under a curse; that is, whether the city and its wall, which was just then undergoing fundamental repair, were secure! What a monstrous idea! As far as we younger ones were concerned, Troy, the city, and everything its name implied, had grown out of this hill, Ate, and we could not imagine it being anywhere else on earth but here, in view of Mount Ida, before the glittering plain and the sea gulf with its natural harbour. And the wall, both protective and confining, had grown along with the city: in ancient times the gods themselves, Apollo, Poseidon, had helped to build it so that it would be indestructible, impregnable. Those were the things we said, and as I listened avidly, I also heard the rejoinder: what! Suppose Cousin Lampos simply forgot to ask the Pythia about Troy's paramount concerns because of a passion for Panthous, priest of Apollo? So that the wall, made fast without the blessing of the mighty oracle, was by no means impregnable, but on the contrary, vulnerable? With the Scaean Gate as its vulnerable point? And what about Panthous? Had he perhaps followed our rather unprepossessing cousin across the sea voluntarily, not as a captive? And Priam had been weak enough to dedicate the foreigner as the priest of Apollo, which after all could mean nothing else but that we acknowledged the sovereignty of Delphi in matters of religion? Or at least in matters concerning this one god, Apollo?

All this was so incredible. So ridiculous. Such a poor invention that I, a child, could only beg them to spare me any more. Yet the subject nagged at me, made me so keen for every scrap of conversation where it flared up that again and again I felt impelled to force my way into the circle of my elders, to sneak between Hector's already powerful thighs, crouch there leaning against him, and drink in every word. It was not my birth that made me a Trojan, it was the stories told in the inner courts. I stopped being one when I was caged in the basket, as I heard the whisper of the mouths at the peephole. Now that Troy no longer exists, I am one again: a Trojan woman. And nothing more.

To whom can I tell that?

Yes. My familiarity with the inner courts, with every impulse that stirred there and touched me, the perfect pitch with which I could gauge the whispers which ceaselessly filled them – that was the one advantage I had over Panthous the Greek, at least in the beginning. Did I not even ask him once why he was here – that is there, in Troy? 'Out of curiosity, my dear,' he said in the flippant tone he had acquired. But could anyone leave the oracle at Delphi, the centre of the world, from curiosity? 'Ah, my little infidel!' he said. 'If only you knew what it was like, that centre.' Often he saddled me with names that did not fit me until later on. When I really got to know Troy, *my* centre, I understood what he meant. It was not curiosity that would have driven me away, but horror. But where was there a place left to go, and in what ship?

I really do not know why Panthous preoccupies me so. Is it that some word, linked to his name, is trying to free itself from depths to which I have not descended? Or is it an image? An image from long, long ago that is floating and that perhaps I can capture if I let my attention wander quietly where it will. I look downhill. What looks like a procession of people, their faces uplifted, densely packed in the narrow street below me. Threatening, avid, wild. Get it in focus. Get it in focus. Yes: the still, white centre. A boy clad all in white, leading the young white bull by a cord. The untouchable white spot in all the turbulence. And the heated face of my nurse, holding me on her arm. And Panthous. But I do not see that, I know it: Panthous at the head of the procession, little more than a boy himself, very young, they say very handsome. And he will lead the crowd to the Scaean Gate and slaughter the bull, but release the boy. Henceforth the god Apollo, protector of the city, wanted no more boy sacrifices, he said. 'Boy sacrifice,' that's the term. I never saw another boy sacrifice in Troy, although . . . Priam, my father, needed Panthous in order to abolish this sacrifice. And when the Greeks charged the Scaean Gate in the ninth year of the war and threatened to capture it – the gate where the Greek had kept a boy from being sacrificed – then people said: 'Panthous the traitor.' My innocent, credulous people. In the end I no longer liked Panthous. I did not like the thing in me which he had been able to seduce.

Who lives will see. It occurs to me that secretly I am tracking the story of my fear. Or more precisely, the story of its unbridling: more precisely still, of its setting free. Yes, it's true, fear too can be set free, and that shows that it belongs with everything and everyone who is oppressed. The king's daughter is not afraid, for fear is weakness and weakness can be amended by iron discipline. The madwoman is afraid, she is mad with fear. The captive is supposed to be afraid. The free woman learns to lay aside her unimportant fears and not to fear the one big important fear because she is no longer too proud to share it with others. Formulas, granted.

No doubt people are right when they say that the closer you come to death, the closer and brighter are the pictures of childhood and youth. An eternity has passed since I looked at them. How difficult it was after all – almost impossible – to see the SECOND SHIP for what Hecuba exclaimed it really was: a game of fear. What was at stake? Was it so important for them to send men like Anchises, like Calchas the seer on the ship? Anchises, who had grown old by the time he returned. Calchas, who did not come back at all. All right, so there was the matter of the king's sister Hesione. 'Hesione,' my father Priam said in the assembly, speaking in a lachrymose, pathetic tone, 'Hesione, the king's sister, held by the Spartan Telamon, who has taken her by force.' The men in the council looked perplexed. 'Now, now, "held,"' mocked Hecuba, '"taken by force."' After all, Hesione was not being treated like a humble captive in Sparta, was she? If our information was correct, had Telamon not made her his wife? Made her the queen? That wasn't the point, he said. 'A king who does not try to win back his sister when she is abducted loses face.' 'Oh,' said Hecuba sarcastically. That was all that was said in public. They quarrelled in their megaron, and the worst part was that my father sent me out. His ambivalent feelings transferred themselves to me, condensed into a sensation which seemed to reside in my navel: a vibrating tension which Parthena, my nurse, taught me to call 'fear.' 'You mustn't be so afraid, little daughter. The child has too much imagination.'

Banners, waving, cheers, sparkling water, gleaming oars – fifty *oars*, the palace scribes entered on their clay tablets; they did not know how to do anything but count – as the SECOND SHIP left port. Those who stayed behind shouted inflammatory slogans to the men who stood on board the ship: 'The king's sister or death!' Beside me stood Aeneas, who shouted up to his father: 'Hesione or death!' I was horrified and knew that I was not allowed to be horrified. Aeneas was acting in the interests of the royal family, of which I was a member, when he wished death upon his father for the sake of a woman who just happened to be the king's sister. I suppressed my horror and forced myself to admire Aeneas. It was then that my ambivalent feelings began. So did Aeneas's – he told me later. He told me that the longer the action to recapture the strange woman continued, the more indifferent he became to her fate, indeed the more he downright detested her; while at the same time his concern for his father grew and grew. I had no way of knowing that. It was then – yes, it must have been then that those dreams began in which Aeneas appeared to me, in which I felt pleasure when he threatened me. Dreams which tormented me and drove me into a state of indelible guilt, a desperate self-estrangement. Oh yes, no doubt I could supply some particulars about the origin of dependency and fear. But no one is going to ask me.

I wanted to become a priestess. I wanted the gift of prophecy, come what may.

We swiftly varied our mistaken judgments to avoid seeing the sinister reality behind the glorious façade. One example enraged me when I was still capable of feeling enraged: all the Trojans had cheered just as I did when the SECOND SHIP set sail, yet later they insisted that this ship was the beginning of our downfall. How could they have forgotten so quickly what they had learned at the knees of their mothers and nurses just as I did: the chain of events ruinous to our city stretched back to remotest antiquity. Destruction, rebuilding, and destruction again, under the sovereignty of a shifting succession of kings, most of them luckless. So what made people hope, what made us all hope that this particular king, my father Priam specifically, would break the chain of misfortune; that he would be the one to restore the Golden Age? Why are we carried away by the very wishes that are grounded in error? The thing they resented most about me later on was my refusal to give in to their disastrous wishful thinking. This refusal (not the Greeks) cost me my father, mother, brothers and sisters, friends, my people. And won me what? No, I will postpone thinking of my joys until I need to.

When the SECOND SHIP returned at last, without the king's sister of course (suddenly everyone was saying 'of course'!), and without Calchas the seer either; when the people gathered in the harbour, disappointed and it seemed to me almost hostile, grumbling because they had learned that the Spartan had laughed at the Trojans' demand; when the dark shadow appeared on my father's brow – I cried in public for the last time. Hecuba, who did not exult to see her dire prediction confirmed, reprimanded me for it, not harshly, but firmly. One did not cry over political events. Tears clouded one's reasoning powers. If our opponent gave in to his feelings – if he laughed! – so much the worse for him. It had been clear to everyone who had all his wits about him that we would not see my father's sister again. Naturally the common people attached high-flown expectations, and suffered inevitable disappointments, at every ship that came and went. Their rulers had to control themselves. I rebelled against my mother's rules. In retrospect I see she took me seriously. My father only looked to me for consolation. I never again cried in public. And less and less often in private.

There was still the question of Calchas the seer. Where was he? Had he died on the journey? No. Had he been killed? Not that either. So he was held hostage by the Greeks? Let the people believe that if they liked (and in fact they did believe it for a time): no harm in confirming the bad reputation of the Greeks. Different tidings ran through the corridors of the palace. When they were reported to me I clenched my fists and resentfully refused to believe it. Marpessa stuck to her story. It was the truth, she said, they had talked about it in the council. And not only that, in the king and queen's bedchamber, too. What, Calchas had gone over to the Greeks? Our highly respected seer, who was privy to the innermost state secrets, was a deserter? 'Yes, that's it exactly.' The report had to be false. Furious, I went to Hecuba, unburdened my conscience without thinking about what I was doing, forced my mother to take action. Marpessa vanished from sight. Parthena, my nurse, appeared with tear-stained, reproachful eyes. A ring of silence descended around me. The palace, the place I called home, drew away from me; the inner courtyards I loved stopped speaking to me. I was alone with my justice.

The first cycle.

It was Aeneas – Aeneas, whom I always believed because the gods neglected to give him the ability to lie – who confirmed it all, word for word: yes, Calchas the seer had stayed with the Greeks by his own wish. Aeneas had this on reliable evidence, from Anchises, his father, who had aged by many years. Calchas the seer was afraid that now that the SECOND SHIP had failed, the Trojans would call him to account for the favourable prophecies he had made before it sailed: so hopelessly banal were the reasons for far-reaching decisions! And the odd thing about it, Anchises had told Aeneas, was that the royal family had forced Calchas to make these favourable predictions. Without benefit of a seer.

I had known from the beginning that Marpessa was telling the truth. 'Not only that,' I heard myself tell Aeneas, 'I myself knew from the start.' The voice that said this was a stranger's voice, and of course today I know – I have known for a long time – that it was no accident that this strange voice which had stuck in my throat many times already in the past should speak out of me for the first time in Aeneas's presence. I set it free deliberately so that it would not tear me apart; I had no control over what happened next. 'I knew it, I knew it': over and over in this alien, high-pitched, moaning voice from which I had to get away to safety; so that I had to cling to Aeneas, who was shocked but held his ground. Held his ground, oh,

Aeneas. Tottering, limbs shaking, I clung to him; each of my fingers followed its own inclinations, gripped and tore at his clothing; my mouth, as it expelled the cry, also produced a foam that settled on my lips and chin; and my legs, which were as much out of my control as all my other limbs, jerked and danced with a disreputable, unseemly delight that I myself did not feel in the least. They were out of control, everything in me was out of control, I was uncontrollable. Four men could scarcely hold me.

Strange to say, a spark of triumph lit my way into the darkness where I tumbled at last: strange to those who do not know what cunning compacts link illness to suppressed manifestations. So this was the seizure; and for a while my life divided itself into the time before the seizure and the time after the seizure – a chronology which soon became invalid like almost all those which followed. For weeks I could not stand up or stir a limb. Wanted to be unable to stand or stir. 'Let Marpessa come': that was the first order I was able to give. Above me Hecuba's mouth said: 'No.' Then I let myself sink back into the darkness. In some way I had control of the rising and sinking of this hard, heavy structure, my consciousness. The undecided part was: would I – who, I? – rise to the surface again? I kept myself in suspension, a pain-free state. Once when I bobbed up, it was Marpessa's face that hung over me, her hand that bathed my temples with diluted wine. That was painful, for in this case I had to stay. Marpessa had grown thin and pale and silent like me. I did not lose consciousness completely again. I consented to be helped. I got well, as people call it. I longed for the office of the priesthood the way a shipwrecked sailor longs for land. I did not want the world the way it was, but I wanted to serve devotedly the gods who ruled it. My wish held a contradiction. I gave myself some time before I noticed it; I have always granted myself these times of partial blindness. To become seeing all of a sudden – that would have destroyed me.

For example, it was not until that dark, stormy night on the sea voyage here, when everything was coming to an end, that I was able to ask Marpessa what they did to her when they took her away. 'Nothing special,' she said. 'They sent me to the stables.' 'To the stables!' 'Yes.' As a horse maid among the stable-hands drawn from a dozen tribes. Everyone knew what things were like in the stables. I could imagine why Marpessa never let a man near her again. When I entrusted her with my twins, that was a kind of atonement which could neither increase her devotion to me nor soften her implacability. She always let me feel that there was no way I could make amends to her. The fact that she understood me made things worse. The palace scribe and the young slave girl, Hecuba's servant, from whom Marpessa had learned the truth about Calchas the seer, had left with the next prisoner transport which

King Priam sent to the King of the Hittites. After that no one spoke the name of Calchas, either in praise or in blame.

How often what I fervently desired has fallen to me when I no longer desired it. Marpessa has freely expressed her affection for me ever since I was raped right before her eyes by Ajax, whom the Greeks call Ajax the Lesser. If I am not mistaken I heard her cry: 'Take me!' But she understands perfectly well that I no longer court anyone's love or friendship. No.

One should not strive to unite the incompatible. Hecuba warned me about that early on; to no avail, of course. 'Your father,' she said, 'wants it all, and all at the same time. He wants the Greeks to pay for permission to bring their goods through our Hellespont: right. He thinks that in return they should respect King Priam: wrong. Why should it hurt him that they laugh at him when they think they are superior? Let them laugh, as long as they pay. And you, Cassandra,' Hecuba said to me, 'make sure that you do not burrow too deep into your father's soul.'

I am very tired. I have not had a solid sleep for weeks. Incredible, but I could fall asleep now. After all, I can no longer afford to postpone anything, not even sleep. It's not good to be overtired when you die. People say that the dead sleep, but it isn't true. Their eyes stand open. The wide-open eyes of my dead brothers, which I closed, beginning with Troilus. The eyes of Penthesilea staring at Achilles, Achilles

the brute, they must have driven him crazy. My
father's open, dead eyes. I did not see the eyes of my
sister Polyxena in death. When they dragged her away
to Achilles' grave, she had the look that only dead
people have. Is it a consolation that Aeneas's eyes
will not find death but sleep for many nights to come?
Not a consolation. A knowledge. The only words I
have left are uncoloured by hope or dread.

When the queen walked out the gate a little while
ago, I let myself feel a last tiny hope that I could get
her to spare the children's lives. All I had to do was to
look into her eyes. She was doing what she had to do.
She did not make things as they are, she is adapting to
things as they are. Either she gets rid of her husband,
this empty-headed ninny, and makes a good job of it,
or she gives up herself: her life, her sovereignty, her
lover – who, if I interpret the figure in the background
correctly, also looks to be a self-centred ninny, but
young, handsome, smooth-fleshed. She indicated to
me with a shrug of her shoulders that what was
happening had nothing to do with me personally. In
different times nothing would have prevented us from
calling each other sister. That is what I read in my
adversary's face, where Agamemnon, the imbecile, was
meant to see love and devotion and the joy of reunion;
and in fact he did see them. Whereupon he stumbled
up the red carpet like an ox to the slaughterhouse.
Both of us had this same thought, and the same smile
appeared in the corners of Clytemnestra's mouth as

in mine. Not cruel. Painful. Pain that fate did not put us on the same side. I credit her with knowing that she, too, will be stricken with the blindness that comes with power. She, too, will fail to see the signs. Her house, too, will fall.

It took me a long time to understand that. Not everyone could see what I saw. Not everyone perceived the naked, meaningless shape of events. I thought they were making fun of me; but they believed what they were saying. There must be a meaning in that. What if we were ants. The entire race plunges blindly into the ditch, drowns, forms the bridge for the few survivors who are the germ of the new race. Like ants we walk into every fire. Every water. Every river of blood. Simply in order not to have to see. To see what, then? Ourselves.

As if I had unchained a boat in calm water, it drifts incessantly in the current, first forward, then back. When I was a child. When I was a child I had a brother named Aisakos whom I loved more than anything, and he loved me. The only thing he loved more than me was his beautiful young wife, Asterope, and when she died in childbirth, he could no longer live either and he jumped off the cliffs into the sea; but his guards rescued him time after time. Until once he really did sink under the waves and was not found until a black diving bird with a red throat appeared at the place where he had dived into the sea. Calchas, the interpreter of omens, recognised the transformed shape of Aisakos, and the bird was immediately taken under public protection. I alone – how could I forget it; that was the first time! – I alone spent days and nights writhing in my bed, convulsed with weeping. Even if I could have believed (but I did not) that my brother Aisakos was a bird; that the goddess Artemis, who was credited with some peculiar behaviour, had transformed him, thus granting his most heartfelt desire – I did not want a bird in place of my brother. I wanted him, Aisakos, the sturdy, warm-skinned man with the curly brown hair who used to treat me differently from all my brothers in the palace. Who used to carry me on his shoulders, not just through all the courtyards, but also through the streets of the city that had been built around the citadel; which now is destroyed like the citadel; and where all the people used to greet him who now are dead or captive. Who used to call me 'my poor little sister' and to take me out into open country where the sea breeze swept through the olive trees, making the leaves glint silver so that it hurt me to look at them. Who finally took me along to the village on the slopes of Mount Ida where he had his home: for although his father was Priam, his mother was Arisbe. Back then she seemed to me ancient and sinister, too. I saw her white eyes flash out of the darkness of a small room hung with herbs while Asterope, Aisakos's slender young wife, greeted her husband with a smile that cut into my flesh. I wanted him back, skin, hair,

and all, I screamed: 'Him, him, him, him.' Aisakos.
Moreover, I never wanted to have a child; but I did
not say that, I only thought it.

Yes, it was then that I heard them say for the first
time: 'She is out of her mind.' Hecuba, my mother,
pressed my twitching, quaking shoulders against the
wall with arms that had a man's strength. Forever the
twitching of my limbs, forever the cold hard wall
against them, life against death, my mother's strength
against my weakness; forever a slave woman holding
my head and forever the bitter brown juice which
Parthena, my nurse, poured down my throat; forever
the heavy sleep and the dreams. The child of Asterope
and Aisakos who had died with his mother at birth
was growing inside me. When it was fully developed I
did not want to bring it into the world, so I spat it out,
and it was a toad. It disgusted me. Merops, the ancient
interpreter of dreams, listened to me attentively. Then
he recommended to Hecuba that she remove from her
daughter's proximity all men who resembled Aisakos.
What could he be thinking of, I was told Hecuba
asked the old man in fury. He shrugged his shoulders
and went away. Priam sat down by my bed and discussed affairs of state with me in all seriousness. It
was a shame, he said, a crying shame, that I could not
take his place and sit in the high-backed chair at the
council next morning dressed in his clothes. I loved
my father even more than usual when he worried
about me. Everyone in the palace knew that he took

problems personally: I considered that a strength; everyone else considered it a weakness. Then it became a weakness.

The sequence of images moves with frantic speed through my tired head; words cannot keep up with them. Strange, the similarity of the tracks in my memory, no matter how varied the recollections that lead to them. These figures which light up over and over like signal fires. Priam, Aisakos, Aeneas, Paris. Yes. Paris. Paris and Operation THIRD SHIP, each of whose presuppositions and consequences is clear to me, whereas at the time I was all but lost in impenetrable chaos. The THIRD SHIP. They were fitting out the ship at the very time I was preparing for my dedication as a priestess. Perhaps this explains why I identified with the ship, why I secretly connected my fate with the ship's fate. What I would have given to be able to sail with it. Not just because I knew that this time Aeneas would accompany his father Anchises on the journey; not just because the goal of the expedition blurred over and over whenever one tried to get a clear look at it, and so left ample scope for miraculous expectations – no: I was stirred up, ready for anything because of the gradual, toilsome disclosure of the most delicate points of our family history; because of the unexpected appearance of a long-lost, unknown brother. I cared – once again I cared far too much – for the strange young man who turned up all of a sudden to take part in the festival games played in memory of a nameless brother who died as a child. I did not have to know who he was in order to tremble at the sight of him; his beauty burned me unbearably; I closed my eyes so as not to be exposed to it any longer. I wanted him to win all the competitions! He did win them all: the boxing match, the first footrace, then the second, which my envious brothers had forced more than asked him to run. I placed the wreath on his head, I would not let them refuse me that right. My whole being went out to him. He did not notice. His face seemed veiled as if only his body were present and obedient to his wishes, not his mind. He was a stranger to himself. Now that I think of it, that did not change, no, that did not change. But was this self-estrangement of a prince the key to a great war? I fear that is how people will explain it. They need personal reasons of that kind.

I was in the middle of the arena, and so I only heard reports of what was going on outside meanwhile: the royal guards were sealing off all the exits – for the first time we heard that a young officer named Eumelos had distinguished himself by his caution and consistency during this action – and strict controls were being used. Inside, I saw from close up how Hector and Deiphobus, my two eldest brothers, charged the stranger with drawn swords; he looked more amazed than frightened. Did he really not understand that the order of the victors in the games was pre-established; that he had violated a law? He did not understand.

Then a piercing voice rose above the threatening hum that swelled through the arena: 'Priam! This man is your son.' And in the same moment – who knows why – I knew that it was the truth. Only then came the gesture from my father that immobilised my brothers' swords. My rigid mother nodded after the old shepherd had showed her some swaddling clothes. And the stranger's modest reply when the king asked him his name: 'Paris.' Suppressed laughter from my sisters and brothers: our new brother was called 'bag,' 'pouch.' Yes, the old shepherd said, named after the bag in which he had carried the wee infant son of the king and queen around in the mountains. He produced the bag; it was as old as he, if not older. Then, in one of those abrupt reversals which are typical (*were* typical) of public events in Troy, the triumphal procession to the palace with Paris at the centre. Hold on. Didn't this procession resemble the other one, centred on the white-clad boy sacrifice? Once again I was mute amid the excitedly chattering crowd of my sisters; galled and sore, torn open.

I was desperate to find out all about it this time, because it had to do with Paris. I believe I actually said so. How embarrassing. Well. Later I no longer believed that events owed it to me to reveal themselves. In those early years I used to chase after them.

Tacitly assuming that all doors and all mouths would spring open to King Priam's daughter. But the place I came to had no doors, only animal hides stretched across the entrances of cave-like dwellings. Moreover, my training in good manners prevented me from subjecting to a pressing interrogation the three mid-wives, ancient and shaggy crones, who had pulled Paris (and indeed almost all of Hecuba's children) from his mother's womb. I would have turned around and gone home if it had not been for Marpessa, who had led me there; I would have been ashamed to have her see me. This was the first time I had a close view of the cave dwellings along the steep bank of our river, the Scamander; of the motley folk encamped at the entrances, dotting the bank, washing their clothes in the river; heaven knows what they lived on. I walked through their midst as if through an aisle of silence that did not feel threatening, only alien; whereas Marpessa hurled greetings in every direction, and from every side cries greeted her. Among them the obscene phrases of men, which she would have answered sharply in the citadel; but here she gave a laughing retort. Can the king's daughter envy a slave girl? Well might I ask such questions. I still do. I saw that the most beautiful thing about Marpessa was the way she walked. She moved her legs with a vigorous motion from the hip, effortlessly, her back erect. Her dark hair worn up in two braids. She also knew the girl who looked after the three ancient mothers.

Oenone, a young creature of conspicuous charm even for this area, famed for the beauty of its women. 'By the Scamander': that was a byword among the young men of the palace when the time came to have their first girl. I had picked it up from my brothers.

Proudly I told the three midwives my real name; Marpessa had advised me against it. What, were these three old women trying to make a fool of me? Oh, the three old sluts. 'A son of Priam?' Ha, they had brought dozens of them into the world, they said. 'Nineteen,' I corrected them: in those days I still set store by family honour. The old crones disputed the number, even debated among themselves. 'But they don't know how to count,' Oenone protested, laughing. Oenone, Oenone, hadn't I heard that name before? Who was it that said it? A man's voice. Paris. Hadn't I already run into her in the palace? Whenever I left the boundaries of the citadel I got into unfathomable, often mortifying situations like this. More harshly than necessary I asked the mothers their opinion: why, of the dozens of Priam's sons, was one in particular not supposed to have been reared? Not reared? The three old hypocrites seemed not even to know what the word meant. Oh no, certainly not. Not in their time. Not that they knew of. Until I heard one of them murmur almost dreamily: 'Yes, if only Aisakos were alive!' 'Aisakos?' I pursued it quick as a flash. Silence multiplied by three. Oenone too was silent. Marpessa was silent.

She was – what am I thinking, she *is!* – the most
silent person in my life.

It was the same at the palace. A palace of silence.
Hecuba, stifling her rage, was silent. Parthena the
nurse, showing her fear openly, was silent. I learned a
lot by observing the various types of silence. Only
much later did I learn silence myself; what a useful
weapon. I turned and twisted the only word I knew:
Aisakos, until suddenly one night a second name
dropped out of it: Arisbe. Hadn't she been Aisakos's
mother? Was she still alive?

For the first time I had experience of a lesson that I
often put to the test later on: forgotten people know
about each other. Not quite by chance I met the
clever Briseis – daughter of the renegade seer Calchas,
who had turned into one of the forgotten overnight –
outside the gates of Troy at the great autumn market,
which was a flourishing centre of east–west trade; and
stupidly asked her whether she still knew who I was.
Who did not know who I was? Briseis had set out her
particularly glowing textile goods. She, who even in
the past had been highly independent and impulsive,
left her customers standing while she described to
me, readily and impersonally, where I might find
Arisbe: at the same market, in the potters' row. I
went there, questioned no one, looked at people's
faces: Arisbe looked like an older Aisakos. Scarcely
had I approached her than she murmured that I
should visit her in her hut at such-and-such a spot at

the foot of Mount Ida. So she had been told that I was coming. So my every step was being observed. I did not even notice Priam's guards, who were following me; I was a stupid young thing. The first time they were pointed out to me – by Panthous the Greek, of course – I got on my high horse, ran to my father: encountered the king, the mask. Men keeping watch on me? He asked. Wherever did I get such an idea? The young lads were there to protect me. He, not I, must be allowed to decide whether I needed them. Those who had nothing to hide had no reason to fear the eye of the king.

As far as I know I was alone when I went to visit Arisbe.

Once again this by-world, counter-world in the environs of the city which, unlike the stone world of palace and town, grew rankly and proliferated like a plant, lush, carefree, as if it did not need the palace, as if it lived with its back turned to the palace, and to me, too. People knew who I was, greeted me imperturbably, but I returned their greeting a shade too quickly. It humiliated me to go there seeking information the palace denied me. 'Denied': I thought of it that way for a long time until I understood that they could not deny what they did not have. They did not even understand the questions to which I was seeking an answer, questions which increasingly were destroying my intimate relations with the palace, with my family. I realised this too late. The alien being who wanted to know had already eaten its way too deep inside me; I could no longer get rid of it.

Arisbe's hut: how wretched, how small. Was this where big strong Aisakos had lived? The aromatic fragrances, the clusters of herbs along ceiling and walls, a steaming brew on the open fire in the centre of the room. The flames flickered and smoked; apart from that there was darkness. Arisbe was neither friendly nor unfriendly; but I was accustomed to friendliness and still needed it. Unhesitatingly she gave me the information I asked for. Yes: it was Aisakos my half-brother, the divinely blessed seer, who had prophesied, before the birth of the boy they called Paris: a curse lies on this child. Aisakos! That same innocuous Aisakos who used to carry me around on his shoulders? Arisbe, unperturbed, went on. But of course the decisive turn had been Hecuba's dream. By Arisbe's account, shortly before Paris was born Hecuba had dreamed that she was giving birth to a stick of firewood from which countless burning serpents crept forth. Calchas the seer interpreted this to mean: the child whom Hecuba was to bear would set fire to all Troy.

Outrageous tidings. What kind of place was I living in, then?

Arisbe, the massive woman at the fire who stirred the stinking pot, continued in her trumpet-like voice. Of course Calchas's interpretation did not go un-challenged. She herself was also consulted about this

dream of the pregnant queen. 'By whom?' I inter-
jected hastily, and she replied in passing: 'By
Hecuba.' After thorough deliberation, she said, she
had succeeded in giving the dream a different twist.
'Namely?' I asked abruptly. I felt as if I myself were
dreaming. Hecuba, my mother, had had frightening
dreams, had bypassed the official oracle to consult
the former concubine of her husband, the king? Were
they all crazy? Or changelings, as I had so often feared
when I was a child? 'Namely,' said Arisbe, 'that this
child could be intended to restore her rights to the
snake goddess as guardian of the hearth fire in every
home.' My scalp crawled: I must be listening to
something dangerous. Arisbe smiled, then her
resemblance to Aisakos became painful. She did not
know, she said, whether her interpretation had
pleased King Priam. With this enigmatic remark she
sent me away. How much had to come to pass before
this hut became my true home.

Now I had to apply to my father, after all. Things
had reached such a pass that I had to have myself
announced first like everyone else. One of the young
men who had been following me around for weeks
now stood silent and in plain view outside Priam's
door. What was his name? Eumelos? 'Yes,' said
Priam. 'A capable man.' He put on a busy air. For the
first time it occurred to me that the intimacy between
us was based, as is so often the case between men
and women, on the fact that I knew him and he did

not know me. He knew his ideal of me; that was supposed to hold still. I had always liked to see him working at full swing; but not insecure, and hiding his insecurity behind bustling activity. Challengingly I mentioned Arisbe's name. Priam snapped: was his daughter plotting against him? There had already been one female intrigue in the palace, back in the days before Paris was born. One faction had implored him to get rid of the dangerous child. The other, Hecuba among them of course, wanted to save it on the grounds that this particular son was destined for higher things. 'Higher things! That meant he was destined to pretend to his father's throne, what else?'

This sentence tore a veil from my eyes. At last I understood the taciturn or disconcerted looks I had picked up as a child, the ring of rejection – indeed of abhorrence – surrounding my father, which I deliberately broke through: his favourite daughter! The estrangement from my mother, the hardening of Hecuba. And so? Paris was alive. 'Yes,' said Priam. 'The shepherd could not bear to kill him. I'll bet he was bribed by the women. No matter. Better that Troy should fall than that my miraculous son should die.'

I was puzzled. Why was he ruffling up his feathers? And why should Troy fall if Paris lived? And was the king really not able to tell the difference between the tongue of an infant and the dog's tongue which the shepherd brought him as evidence that the child was dead? A flustered messenger announced the arrival of

Menelaus, King of Sparta. So it was his ship that we had seen approaching since dawn. Hecuba entered on state business, seemed not to see me. 'Menelaus. Do you know about it? Maybe it's not such a bad thing.'

I left. While the palace was doing its best to welcome the guest who, strange to say, had come to offer sacrifice at two of our hero graves in order to halt the plague in Sparta; while the temples of all the gods were getting ready for state ceremonies, I was nursing my cross-grained satisfaction. With satisfaction I felt the coldness spreading through me. I did not yet know that not to feel is never a step forward, scarcely a relief. How long it was before feelings once again flooded the desolate rooms of my soul. My rebirth restored the present to me, what people call life, but not only that. It also opened up the past to me, a past that was new, undistorted by hurt feelings, likes and dislikes, and all the luxury emotions that belonged to Priam's daughter. I sat swollen with triumph at the banquet in the place where it behoved me to sit in the ranks of my brothers and sisters. Anyone who had been deceived as I had owed them nothing more. I had had a right to know, I more than anyone. In future I had to know more than they did in order to punish them. Become a priestess in order to gain power? Ye gods. You had to drive me to this extremity to wring this simple sentence from me. What a hard time sentences have had till the end, when they tackle me. How much faster and more easily the sentences get through when they are aimed at others. Arisbe told me so point-blank one time. 'When was that, Marpessa?'

'In the middle of the war,' she says. We women had been meeting for a long time already, outside the caves on the slopes of Mount Ida in the evening. The ancient midwives were still alive, too, and used to cackle with their toothless mouths; and even you smiled back then, Marpessa, at my expense. I was the only one who did not laugh. My old sense of injury swelled inside me. Then Arisbe said that instead of making faces I ought to be delighted that there were people who told me their opinion bluntly. What other daughter from a powerful family was so lucky? 'Quite true,' I said, 'so let it pass.' I believe I loved Arisbe's sense of humour more than anything. It was an unforgettable sight when her powerful body crouched on the rotting tree trunk in front of the cave while she beat time for us with her stick. Who would believe us, Marpessa, if we told them that in the middle of the war we used to meet regularly outside the fortress on paths known to no one but us initiates? That we, far better informed than any other group in Troy, used to discuss the situation, confer about measures (and carry them out, too); but also to cook, eat, drink, laugh together, sing, play games, learn? Always months came when the Greeks, entrenched behind their seafront palisades, did not attack. It even proved possible to hold the Great Market outside the gates of Troy, under the noses of the Greek fleet. And not seldom one of their princes – Menelaus, Agamemnon, Odysseus, or one of the two Ajaxes – would turn up among the stalls and booths, grab at our wares, which often were unfamiliar to him, and buy fabrics, leather goods, utensils, and spices for himself or his wife. When Clytemnestra appeared a little while ago, I recognised her at once by her dress. A slave was carrying the fabric for this dress in the wake of the unhappy Agamemnon the first time I saw him at our market. Something about his manner displeased me at once. He pushed his way imperiously to the front of Arisbe's stall, slid the ceramics back and forth choosily, and broke one of the most beautiful vases, which he paid for in haste at a word from Arisbe; then fled with his retinue amid the laughter of the onlookers. He had seen that I had seen him.

'He will take revenge, that one,' I said to Arisbe; and it troubled me deeply that the great and famous commander in chief of the Greek fleet was a weakling who lacked self-esteem. How much better it is to have a strong enemy. Sometimes a minor trait throws light on great events. Suddenly it was clear to me that the report by a Greek deserter (which Priam had ordered not to be circulated further lest our people regard the enemy as a monster) might and must be true: this same Agamemnon had caused his own daughter, a young girl named Iphigenia, to be sacrificed on the altar of the goddess Artemis before his fleet crossed over. How often I was compelled to think of Iphigenia all through the war years. The only conversation I consented to have with this man was about his daughter. It was on board the ship, the day after the storm. I was standing at the stern, he was beside me. Deep blue sky and the line of white foam which the ship left in the smooth blue-green sea. I asked Agamemnon point-blank about Iphigenia. He wept, but not the way people weep from grief: from fear and weakness. He had to do it, he said. 'Had to do what?' I asked coldly. I wanted him to say it. He squirmed. He had to sacrifice her, he said. That was not what I wanted to hear: but of course murderers and butchers do not know words like 'murder' and 'butcher.' How far I had removed myself from them even in my speech. 'Your Calchas' (Agamemnon said accusingly) 'absolutely demanded this sacrifice from me if we were to have favourable winds.' 'And you believed him,' I said. 'Maybe I didn't,' he whined. 'No, I didn't. It was the others, the princes. They were all envious of me, the commander in chief. They were all spiteful. What can a leader do against a host of superstitious men?' 'Leave me in peace,' I said. The vengeance of Clytemnestra rose up huge before me.

Long ago, after my first encounter with this man of ill omen, I told Arisbe: 'No priest could have gotten Priam to make such a sacrifice.' Arisbe stared at me wide-eyed; then I thought of Paris. Was it the same thing? Was it really the same thing: to have an infant child killed secretly, or to butcher a grown girl in public? And did I fail to see that it was the same thing because not I the daughter was affected but Paris the son? 'You're slow on the uptake, my dear,' said Arisbe.

I was slow on the uptake. My privileges intruded between me and the most necessary insights; so did my attachment to my own family, which did not depend on the privileges I enjoyed. I was almost shocked to find I felt embarrassed by the haughty, affected behaviour of the royal family when we walked in solemn procession, in company with our guest Menelaus, to bring Pallas Athena her new robe. Beside me walked Panthous; I saw him smile mockingly. 'Are you laughing at the king?' I asked him sharply. Then for the first time I saw something like fear in his eyes. And I saw that he had a very fragile body topped by a somewhat overlarge head. I understood why he used to call me 'little Cassandra.' At that very moment he stopped doing so. Just as he stopped visiting me at night. For a long time no one visited me at night. I suffered of course, hated myself for the dreams in which I found a perverse relief, until all this extravagant emotion revealed itself for what it was: nonsense, and dissolved away.

Easy to think like that, but what else shall I do now that it's all behind me? The transition from the world of the palace to the world of the mountains and woods was also the transition from tragedy to burlesque, whose essence is that you do not treat yourself as tragic. Important, yes, and why not? But you do not treat yourself as tragic the way the upper echelons in the palace do. The way they must. How else could they persuade themselves that they have a right to their selfishness? How else could they heighten their enjoyment further than by letting it unfold against a background of tragedy? I certainly contributed my bit; all the more credibly because I did it my own way. Madness invading the banquet – what could be more grisly, and hence more stimulating to the appetite? I am not ashamed. Not any more. But neither have I been able to forget it. I was sitting at the royal banquet on the eve of Menelaus's departure, which was also the eve of departure for the THIRD SHIP. On my right was Hector, whom my brothers and sisters and I dubbed 'the Dim Cloud' among ourselves; on my left, stubbornly silent, Polyxena. Across from me sat my charming young brother Troilus with clever Briseis, daughter of the renegade Calchas: the couple had placed themselves under my protection – mine of all people's – which flattered my vanity. At the head of the table were Priam, Hecuba, and Menelaus our guest: henceforth no one was supposed to call him our 'guest-friend.' What? Who had forbidden that! 'Eumelos,' I heard. Eumelos? Who is Eumelos? Oh yes, that man in the council who was now the head of the palace guard. Since when did an officer decide the use of words? Ever since those who styled themselves the 'king's party' began to regard the Spartan Menelaus not as our guest-friend but as a spy or a provocateur. As our future enemy. Ever since they had surrounded him with a 'security net.' A new word. In exchange for it we gave away the old word 'guest-friend.' What do words matter? All of a sudden those of us who persisted in saying 'guest-friend' – including me – found themselves under suspicion. But the palace guard was a small band of men in dress uniform who surrounded the king only on high feast days. This would change, and change radically, Eumelos promised. Who? Eumelos. Those who did not yet know the name were eyed askance. Eumelos, son of a lowly scribe and a slave woman from Crete. Whom everyone – everyone within radius of the palace – was suddenly calling 'capable.' A capable man in the right post. But the capable man had created this post for himself. And so what? Wasn't it always the way! Eumelos's remarks circulated among the civil servants. Tasteless remarks; I exchanged sarcastic comments about them with my brother Troilus and his Briseis. Now I met young men on the streets of Troy wearing the insignia of the palace guard, who behaved differently than our young men were accustomed to behave. Presumptuous. My laughter died away. 'I am foolish enough to think that some men are following me,' I said to Panthous. 'They are foolish enough to follow you,' said Panthous. 'At least when you come to see me.' Panthous the Greek was placed under surveillance, suspected of conspiring with Menelaus the Greek. Anyone who came near him fell into the net. Including me. It seemed incredible: the sky grew dark. Ominous, the empty space that had formed around me.

At the banquet in the evening you could tell the different groups apart just by looking: that was something new. Troy had changed while I was not looking. Hecuba, my mother, was not on Eumelos's side. I saw how her face grew stony whenever he approached her. Aeneas's dearly loved father, Anchises, seemed to be the leader of the opposition party. He spoke amiably and candidly with the exasperated Menelaus. Priam seemed to want to please everyone. But Paris, my beloved brother Paris, already belonged to Eumelos. The slender handsome youth, devoted to the bulky man with a horse face.

Inevitably I have given Paris a lot of thought. Now that I come to think of it, he always hankered for attention. Had to push to get ahead. How his face had changed: it was strained now, a tightening around the nose gave it a strange distorted look. His blond locks among the dark heads of Hecuba's other sons and daughters. Eumelos silenced the whispers about Paris's uncertain parentage by proclaiming that Paris was indeed of royal blood, for he was the son of our revered Queen Hecuba and a god: Apollo. We were all embarrassed by the affected way Paris moved his head whenever anyone alluded to his divine parentage; for in the palace it went without saying that a claim like the divine descent of a human being was intended metaphorically. After all, who did not know that the children born after the ceremonial deflowering of the women in the temple were all divinely descended? Moreover, the palace guard adopted a threatening posture if anyone – be it Hector himself, the heir to the throne – made fun of Paris by continuing to use his nickname: 'Pouch, Pouch.' But ridicule was our favourite party game. So did this mean that we were not allowed to make fun of the plan to hang the dilapidated shepherd's pouch in which the shepherd had carried Paris inside the temple of Apollo along with the god's bow and lyre? No. The priestess Herophile, that thin-lipped, leather-cheeked woman who could not stand me, put a stop to this blasphemy. But Eumelos's troop did manage to arrange for a stuffed she-bear to be set up outside the south gate, through which Paris had re-entered Troy, in token that a she-bear had suckled the royal child Paris when his parents exposed him.

And then there was the way my poor brother needed so many girls. Obviously, all my brothers took the girls they found attractive. In happy times the palace used to run a benevolent commentary on the love affairs of the royal sons; and the girls, generally from the lower classes and slaves to boot, felt neither insulted nor particularly elevated by my brothers' desire for them. Hector, for one, exercised restraint, his huge sluggish body preferred to rest; that is why we all looked on with admiration at the way he trained for the war then, completely against his inclination. And it made no difference to Andromache one way or the other. How he could run – ye gods! – when Achilles the brute chased him around the stronghold.

Not one of us – no seeress, no oracle – even dimly suspected what was in store that evening. The focus of attention was not Eumelos, not Paris, not even our guest Menelaus. The eyes of the palace were trained on Briseis and Troilus, a pair of lovers if ever there was one. No one who looked their way could help smiling. Briseis was Troilus's first love, and no one could doubt him when he said she would also be his last. Briseis, not much older but more mature, seemed scarcely able to credit her good fortune; she had not been in high spirits since her father had left us. On the other hand, Oenone, the supple beauty whose most striking feature was her neck – a swan's neck crowned by a beautifully shaped head – Oenone, whom Paris had brought with him out of the mountains and who was idolised by the people in the kitchen, seemed depressed. She was serving at table, she had been assigned to the royal couple and their guest; I saw that she had to force herself to smile. In the corridor I caught her drinking a goblet of wine in one gulp. I was already beginning to quake inside, I was still suppressing it. I did not deign to look at any of the figures who were loitering in our vicinity but asked Oenone what was wrong. Wine and worry had flushed away her awe of me. Paris was sick, she said, pale-lipped, and none of her remedies could help. Oenone, who, the servants believed, had been a water nymph in her previous life, was versed in all matters of plants and their effects on the human organism; almost everyone in the palace went to her when they were sick. Paris's sickness was unknown to her and made her afraid. He loved her; she had tokens which left her in no doubt of that. But when he was lying in her arms he used to cry out another woman's name: 'Helen, Helen.' He said Aphrodite had promised her to him. But had anyone heard of Aphrodite, our dear goddess of love, driving a woman to a man who does not love her, who does not even know her? Who wants to possess her only because it is claimed that she is the most beautiful woman in the world? Because by possessing her he would become supreme among men?

Behind the trembling voice of Oenone I could hear plainly the hoarse, piercing voice of Eumelos, and the quaking inside me intensified. Like everyone's, my body gave me signs; but unlike others, I was not able to ignore them. Fearing disaster I re-entered the banquet hall, where the one group had grown stiller and stiller while the other – those attached to

Eumelos – had waxed louder and more impudent. Paris, who had drunk too much already, made Oenone give him another cup of wine, which he downed in a gulp. Then in a loud voice he addressed Menelaus the Greek, who sat next to him, on the subject of his beautiful wife, Helen. Menelaus – no longer young, balding, inclined to stoutness, and not looking for a fight – answered his host's son politely until his questions grew so bold that Hecuba, unwontedly angry, ordered her ill-mannered son to keep silent. The hall grew still as death. Only Paris leaped to his feet, shouted: What? He was to keep silent? Again? Still? Demean himself? Make himself invisible if possible? 'Oh no. Those days are past. I, Paris, did not come back in order to keep silent. It is I, Paris, who will fetch the king's sister back from the enemy. But if they refuse to give her to me, I'll find another woman, more beautiful than she. Younger. Nobler. Richer. That's what I have been promised, if you all want to know!'

Never before had such silence reigned in the palace of Troy. Each person present felt that a mark was being overstepped here which had not been violated until now. No member of our family had ever dared to speak in such a way. But I, I alone saw. Or did I really 'see'? What was it, then? I felt. Experienced – yes, that's the word. For it was, it is, an experience when I 'see,' when I 'saw.' Saw that the outcome of this hour was our destruction. Time stood still, I would not wish that on anyone. And the cold of the grave. The ultimate estrangement from myself and from everyone. That is how it seemed. Until finally the dreadful torment took the form of a voice; forced its way out of me, through me, dismembering me as it went; and set itself free. A whistling little voice, whistling at the end of its rope, that makes my blood run cold and my hair stand on end. Which as it swells, grows louder and more hideous, sets all my members to wriggling and rattling and hurling about. But the voice does not care. It floats above me, free, and shrieks, shrieks, shrieks. 'Woe,' it shrieked. 'Woe, woe. Do not let the ship depart!'

Then the curtain fell before my thoughts. The abyss opened. Darkness. I fell headlong. They say I made horrifying gurgling noises, that I foamed at the mouth. At a signal from my mother the guards – Eumelos's men! – gripped me under the shoulders and dragged me out of the hall, where (they tell me) it was so quiet that people could hear my feet scraping on the floor. The temple physicians crowded around me; Oenone was not admitted. I was locked in my room, so they say. At the banquet the stricken company were told that I needed rest. I was bound to recover, the incident was trifling. Lightning swift the rumour spread among my brothers and sisters that I was mad.

It was reported to me that early the next morning the people cheered the departure of Menelaus and, at the same time, the sailing of the THIRD SHIP; and that they crowded around to receive their portion of sacrificial meat and bread. That evening the city was noisy. Not a sound penetrated the inner courtyard onto which my window looked out; all the entryways were barred. The sky I stared at from my window was impenetrably black both day and night. I did not want to eat. Parthena, my nurse, gave me little swallows of asses' milk. I did not want to feed this body. I wanted this criminal body, where the voice of death had its seat, to starve, to wither away. Lunacy: an end to the torture of pretence. Oh, I enjoyed it dreadfully, I wrapped it around me like a heavy cloak, I let it penetrate me layer by layer. It was meat and drink to me. Dark milk, bitter water, sour bread. I had gone back to being myself. But my self did not exist.

To be forced to give birth to what will destroy you: the terror beyond terror. I could not stop producing madness, a pulsating gullet that spat me out, then sucked me in, spat me out, then sucked me in. I had never worked harder than when I could not even move my little finger. I was out of breath, gasped for air, panted. My heart raced and pounded like the hearts of fighters after a match. And there *was* a fight going on inside me, I saw that all right. Two adversaries had chosen the dead landscape of my soul as their battle-field and were engaged in a life-and-death struggle. Only madness stood between me and the intolerable pain which these two would otherwise have inflicted on me, I thought. So I clung to the madness as it clung to me. In my heart of hearts, where the madness did not penetrate, something still knew about the moves and countermoves I allowed myself 'higher up': there is a comic element in all madness. Those who learn to recognise and to use it have won.

Hecuba came, severe. Priam, anxious. My sisters, timid. Parthena, my nurse, sympathetic. Marpessa, reserved. No one was any use. Not to mention the solemn helplessness of Panthous. I let myself sink deeper, experimentally, in tiny thrusts. The tie that bound me to these people was very, very thin; it could tear. A hideous itch. I had to take a chance and give the monstrous apparitions an even wider berth, withdraw my senses even farther. It is not fun, I do not mean to imply that. You pay for journeys to the underworld, which is full of shapes no one is prepared to meet. I howled. Wallowed in my own filth. Scratched up my face, would not let anyone near me. I had the strength of three men – inconceivable what counterforce had subdued it until now. I climbed the cold walls of my room, from which everything had been removed but a pile of twigs. I ate with my fingers like an animal. My hair stood out matted and filthy around my head. No one, including me, knew how it would end. Oh, I was obstinate.

One day a figure entered; I bellowed at it, too. It crept into a corner and stayed there until my voice gave out. A long time after I had grown still, I heard it say: 'This is not the way you can punish them.' These were the first human words I had heard for such a long time, it took me an eternity to understand what they meant. Then I started bellowing again. The figure disappeared. That night, in a lucid moment, I could not decide: had it really been there or was it, too, one of the illusory apparitions that surrounded me? The next day it came again. So it was real. It was Arisbe.

She never repeated what she had said the day before; this was her way of letting me know that she knew I had understood her. I would have liked to strangle her, but she was as strong as I was, and fearless. I noticed that Parthena, my nurse, admitted her secretly. By not betraying her presence I made it clear that I needed her. Apparently she believed it was up to me to free myself from madness. I heaped filthy abuse on her for that. She gripped the hand with which I was trying to strike her and said sternly: 'Enough self-pity.' I was silent at once. People did not talk to me that way.

'Come to the surface, Cassandra,' she said. 'Open your inner eye. Look at yourself.'

I hissed at her like a cat. She left.

So I looked. Not immediately. I waited until it was night. Until I was lying on the crackling twigs, covered with a blanket which Oenone might have woven. So I was allowing names. Oenone. One of *them*. She had played a dirty trick on me, taking my beloved brother away from me, Paris, the handsome blond one. Whom I would have drawn to me if it had not been for the magical arts of this water nymph. Oenone, the filthy beast. Did it hurt? Yes. It hurt. I raised myself a tiny bit closer to the surface, to observe the pain. Groaning, I endured it. I clawed the blankets, I clung to it so that the pain would not wash me away. Hecuba. Priam. Panthous. So many names for deception. For neglect. For lack of appreciation. How I hated them. How I wanted to show them I hated them.

'Fine,' said Arisbe, who was sitting there again. 'And what about your part in it?'

'What do you mean, what about my part in it? Whom have I hurt? I, the weak one? What harm have I done all these people who are stronger than I am?'

'Why did you make them strong?'

I did not understand the question. The part of me that was eating and drinking again, that called itself 'I' again, did not understand the question. The other part, which had been in control during the madness, was no longer being asked; 'I' was suppressing it. Not without regret I let the madness go, not without dismay my inner eye saw an unknown form arising out of the dark waters as they dispersed. The gratitude I owed and showed to Arisbe held more than a grain of ingratitude and rebellion; she seemed to expect that. One day she declared she was no longer needed, and when I told her in a fit of emotion that I would never forget certain things she had done, she replied coolly: 'Yes, you will.' It has always upset me when other people knew more about me, or thought they knew more, than I did.

It took them a long time to make up their minds about me, Arisbe told me years later. Which should they bet on: my inclination to conform with those in power, or my craving for knowledge? 'They!' So 'they' existed, after all, and they were trying to 'make up their minds' about me! 'Don't be childish,' said Arisbe. 'Admit it; for too long you have been trying to have it both ways.'

So that is how it was. At last I was coming back to life, I heard the others say; that meant coming back to them. Into the snare. Into the everyday world of the palace and the temple, whose customs seemed as strange and unnatural to me as if they belonged to an alien race. The first time I caught the blood of a lamb in the sacrificial vessel again at the altar of the Thymbraian Apollo, the meaning of this act completely escaped me; anxious, I believed I was taking part in a sacrilege. 'You have been far away, Cassandra,' said Panthous, who was observing me. 'It's really a pity that when one comes back one always finds the same old thing.' Apart from this moment, apart from this single sentence, he had grown more impenetrable. Quickly I realised why: It was no longer pleasant to be a Greek in Troy.

Eumelos's people were at work. They had won disciples among the palace scribes and the servants in the temple. We must be armed mentally, too, if the Greeks attacked us, they said. Mental armament consisted in defamation of the enemy (people were already talking about the 'enemy' before a single Greek had boarded ship), and in distrust of those suspected of collaborating with the enemy: Panthous the Greek; Briseis, daughter of the renegade Calchas. Who often cried in my bedchamber at night. Even if she was willing to part from Troilus in order not to put him at risk, he would not let her go. All of a sudden I was the protectress of a pair of endangered lovers. The inconceivable happened: my young brother Troilus, the king's son, was treated with hostility because he had chosen the sweetheart he wanted. 'Ye–e–es,' said King Priam, 'too bad, too bad.' Hecuba asked: 'Where do you sleep when the two of them spend the night in your room?' She offered to let me come into her bedchamber. Secretly.

But what kind of place were we living in then? I must try to remember exactly. Did anyone in Troy talk about war? No. He would have been punished. We prepared for war in all innocence and with an easy conscience. The first sign of war: we were letting the enemy govern our behaviour. What did we need him for?

The return of the THIRD SHIP left me strangely cool. Care was taken to see that it arrived at night. Nevertheless, a crowd gathered, torches were raised; but who can recognise faces in dim light, who can count them, who can tell them apart? There, unmistakably, was Anchises, who still moved like a young man until a very advanced age. He seemed in more of a hurry than usual, gave no explanations, refused to let Eumelos accompany him, and disappeared into the palace. There were the young men I should have been waiting for: but for whom was I waiting, really? For Aeneas? For Paris? For which of them did my heart begin to beat faster all the same? No one could get near them. For the first time a broad cordon of Eumelos's men had been thrown around the landing stage. Paris had not come on this ship, we were told next morning at a debriefing for members of the royal family. The Spartans having refused once again to restore the king's sister to him, he had been forced (we heard) to make good his threat. He had, in short, abducted the wife of Menelaus. The wife of the King of Sparta. The most beautiful woman in Greece. Helen. He was travelling with her to Troy by a round-about route.

Helen. The name struck us like a blow. The beautiful Helen. Anything less would not have suited my little brother. We might have known. We had known. I was witness to the scurrying back and forth between the palace and the temple priests, to the sessions of the council that went on day and night; I saw how a news report was manufactured, hard, forged, polished like a spear. At the behest of our dear goddess Aphrodite, the Trojan hero Paris had abducted Helen, the most beautiful woman in Greece, from the boastful Greeks, and so had erased the humiliation once inflicted on our mighty King Priam by the theft of his sister.

The people ran through the streets cheering. I saw a news item turn into the truth. And Priam had a new title: 'our mighty king.' Later, as our prospects of winning the war grew increasingly dim, we had to call him 'our almighty king.' 'Practical reforms,' said Panthous. 'When you have said something long enough, you come to believe it in the end.' 'Yes,' Anchises replied dryly, 'in the *end*.' I hoped at least to impede the language war. I would never say anything but 'Father' or at most 'King Priam.' But I remember quite clearly the dead silence which used to greet such words. 'You can afford to talk like that, Cassandra,' I was told. It was true. What they could afford was to fear murder and homicide less than the sulky eyebrows of their king and the denunciation of Eumelos. I could afford a little foresight and a little defiance. Defiance, not courage.

How long it has been since I thought about the old days. It is true what they say, the approach of death does make your whole life pass before you. Ten years of war. That was long enough to forget completely the question of how the war started. In the middle of a war you think of nothing but how it will end. And put off living. When large numbers of people do that, it creates a vacuum within us which the war flows in to fill. What I regret more than anything else is that, in the beginning, I too gave in to the feeling that for now I was living only provisionally; that true reality still lay ahead of me: I let life pass me by. Panthous started coming to me again, now that I was regarded as cured. I detected in his lovemaking (but I ought not to use the name for the acts he performed on me, they had nothing to do with love) a new trace of subservience which I did not like; and he admitted that before my illness I had not excited him as I did now. I had changed, he said. Aeneas avoided me. 'Of course,' he confessed later, 'you had changed.'

The absent Paris was celebrated in song. Fear lurked inside me. I was not the only one. Unbidden, I interpreted for the king a dream he told at table. Two dragons were fighting. One wore a hammered-gold breastplate, the other carried a sharp, polished spear. Thus the one was invulnerable but unarmed; the other, though armed and hate-filled, was vulnerable. They waged an eternal battle.

'You are in conflict with yourself,' I said to my father. 'You are holding yourself in check. You are paralysing yourself.'

'What are you saying, Priestess?' Priam replied formally. 'Panthous interpreted my dream a long time ago. The dragon in golden armour is me, the king, of course. I must arm myself in order to overcome my treacherous, heavily armed foe. I have already ordered the armourers to step up production.'

'Panthous!' I cried in the temple. 'Well?' he said.

'They are all animals, Cassandra. Half animals, half children. They will obey their appetites no matter what we do. So do we have to stand in their way, let them trample us underfoot? No. I've made my decision.'

'What you decided is to feed the beast in yourself, to arouse it inside you.' His cruel, masklike smile. But what did I know about this man?

You can tell when a war starts, but when does the pre-war start? If there are rules about that, we should pass them on. Hand them down inscribed in clay, in stone. What would they say? Among other things they would say: do not let your own people deceive you.

When Paris finally arrived later (strange to say on an Egyptian ship), he took a heavily veiled woman off board. The people – held back as usual now behind the cordon of Eumelos's soldiers – were silent, holding their breath. The image of the most beautiful woman lit up inside each of them, so radiant that she would blind him if he could see her. Speaking choruses sprang up, first shy, then enthusiastic. 'He-len. He-len,' they said. Helen did not show herself. Nor did she attend the banquet. She was exhausted by the long sea voyage. Paris, a changed man, delivered exquisite gifts given him by his host, the King of Egypt; told miraculous stories. He talked and talked, extravagant, arabesque, with swings which he seemed to consider funny. He laughed many times, he had become a man. I could not take my eyes off him. I could not catch his eyes. Where had his handsome face gotten that crooked line; what sharpness had etched his once soft features?

A sound from the streets penetrated the palace; it was like nothing we had ever heard before, it was like the threatening hum from a beehive when the bees are about to swarm. People's heads were turned by the thought that the beautiful Helen was inside the palace of their king. That night I refused myself to Panthous. Furious, he tried to take me by force. I called for Parthena, my nurse, who was nowhere nearby. Panthous left; he belched lewd insults with a twisted face. The raw flesh beneath the mask. I tried to hide from myself the sorrow that sometimes descended on me, black, from out of the sun.

Every fibre in me shut itself off, refused to recognise that there was no beautiful Helen in Troy. At a time when everyone else in the palace made it clear that they had understood. When I had run into the charming, beautiful-necked Oenone outside Paris's door at dawn, for the second time. When the swarm of legends surrounding Paris's beautiful invisible wife crumbled in embarrassment. When they all lowered their eyes whenever I spoke Helen's name – I was the only one who still did so, saying it over and over as if I could not help myself – and even volunteered to care for her when it was claimed she was still tired. My offer was turned down; and even then I did not yet want to think the unthinkable. 'Really, you're enough to drive one to despair,' Arisbe told me. I grasped at every straw – and a deputation from Menelaus, demanding the return of their queen in no uncertain terms, was hardly a straw. The fact that they wanted her back proved to me that she was here. There was no doubt about my feelings: I wanted Helen to return to Sparta. Yet it was clear to me that the king was bound to reject the demand. With all my heart I wanted to side with him, with Troy. I could not for the life of me see why the debate in the council went on for another whole night. Paris, his face a pale greenish hue, announced in a voice of doom: 'No. We are not going to hand her over.' 'Come on, Paris!' I cried. 'Aren't you happy?' At last his look met mine, confessed to me how he was suffering. This look gave me back my brother.

Then we all forgot the reason for the war. After the crisis in the third year, even the soldiers stopped demanding to see the beautiful Helen. It would have taken more perseverance than a man could muster to go on mouthing a name that tasted increasingly of ashes, gangrene, and decay. They let Helen go and defended their own skins. But they had needed her name in order to cheer for the war. It raised them beyond themselves. 'Notice that,' Aeneas's father Anchises said to us – he enjoyed teaching and, when the end of the war was in sight, forced us to ponder its beginning: 'Notice that they chose a woman. A man could have provided the image of glory and riches just as well. But of beauty? A people who are fighting for beauty!' Paris himself, reluctantly it seemed, had gone to the marketplace and thrown the name of the beautiful Helen to the people. They did not notice that his heart was not in it. I noticed. 'Why do you speak so coldly about your ardent wife?' I asked him. 'My ardent wife?' was his scornful reply. 'Wake up, Sister. Ye gods: she doesn't exist.'

Then my arms jerked up before I even had a chance to realise. Yes, I believed him. I had felt it for a long time, had been eaten up with fear. A seizure, I thought, still clear-headed, but already I could hear that voice saying: 'Woe, woe, woe.' I do not know, did I shriek it aloud or did I only whisper it? 'We are lost. Woe, we are lost!'

I already knew what was going to happen next: the firm grip on my shoulders, the men's hands grabbing me, the clink of metal on metal, the odour of sweat and leather. It was a day like today, an autumn tempest gusting from the sea, driving clouds across the deep blue sky, stones underfoot, laid out just as they are here in Mycenae, the walls of houses, faces, then thicker walls, hardly any people as we approached the palace. Just like here. I felt how a captive feels looking at the citadel of Troy, and ordered myself not to forget it. I did not forget it; but I have not thought about my way there for a very long time. Why not? Maybe because I felt ashamed of my half-deliberate cunning. For when I shrieked, why did I shriek: 'We are lost!'? Why not: 'Trojans, there is no Helen!'? I know why not, I knew even then. The Eumelos inside me forbade me. Eumelos was waiting for me in the palace, it was he at whom I shouted: 'There is no Helen!' But of course he already knew it. The people were the ones I should have told. In other words, I, the seeress, was owned by the palace. And Eumelos was fully aware of that. It enraged me that on top of everything his face could also express mockery and disdain for me. It was for his sake, whom I hated, and for the sake of my father, whom I loved, that I had avoided screaming their state secret out loud. There was a grain of calculation in my self-renunciation. Eumelos saw through me. My father did not.

King Priam felt sorry for himself. This complicated political situation, and now me to boot! He sent the guards away, which was brave of him. If I went on this way he would have no choice but to lock me up, he said wearily. At that, something inside me thought: Not now, not yet. Whatever did I want, for heaven's sake? he asked. All right, so they ought to have talked with me earlier about that confounded business with Helen. All right, so she was not here. The King of Egypt had taken her away from Paris, the stupid boy. Only everyone in the palace knew that, why didn't I? And what were we to do next? How could we get out of the thing without loss of face?

'Father,' I said urgently, in a way I never spoke to

him again. 'No one can win a war waged for a phantom.'

'Why not?' the king asked me in all seriousness. 'Why not? All you have to do is make sure the army does not lose faith in the phantom,' he said. 'And why should there even be a war? You always use these big words. What I think is, we'll be attacked, and what I think is, we'll defend ourselves. The Greeks will ram their heads into a stone wall and withdraw at once. After all, they won't let themselves bleed to death over a woman, no matter how beautiful she is; and I don't believe she is, anyway.'

'And why wouldn't they!' I cried. 'Assuming they believed Helen was with us. Suppose they were the kind of people who could never get over an insult that a woman, be she beautiful or ugly, inflicted on a king, a man?' (As I said that, I was thinking of Panthous, who seemed to hate me since I rejected him. Suppose they were all like that?)

'Don't talk rubbish,' said Priam. 'They want our gold. And free access to the Dardanelles.' 'So negotiate terms!' I suggested. 'That's all we need. To negotiate over our inalienable property and rights!' I began to see that my father was already blind to all the reasons for opposing war, and that what made him blind and deaf was the declaration of the military leaders: we will win. 'Father,' I begged him. 'At least deprive them of the pretext of Helen. Here or in Egypt, she's not worth the life of a single Trojan. Tell that to Menelaus's ambassadors, give them the gifts a host gives guests, and let them go in peace.' 'You must be out of your mind, child,' said the king, genuinely shocked. 'Don't you understand anything any more? The honour of our house is at stake.'

The honour of our house was what concerned me too, I protested. I was thickheaded. I thought that they wanted the same thing I did. So what freedom it brought me the first time I said no, no, I want something different. But on this occasion the king was right to think I meant what I said. 'Child,' he said, drawing me to him; I breathed the scent I loved so much. 'Child. Anyone who does not side with us now is working against us.' Then I promised him to keep secret what I knew about the beautiful Helen, and left unmolested. The guards in the corridor stood motionless. Eumelos bowed as I went past him. 'Bravo, Cassandra,' Panthous said to me in the temple. Now I hated him as he did me. It is too hard to hate oneself. There was a great deal of hate and stifled knowledge in Troy before the enemy, the Greeks, drew all our ill will upon themselves and made us close ranks against them, to begin with.

Over the winter I turned apathetic and silent. I could not say the most important thing, so it no longer occurred to me to say anything. My parents, who no doubt were keeping an eye on me, spoke non-committally to me and each other. Briseis and

Troilus, who continued to solicit my sympathy, did not understand my apathy. Nothing from Arisbe. Nothing from Aeneas. Marpessa mute. No doubt everyone began to give up on me, the inevitable fate of those who give up on themselves. Then in spring the war began as expected.

We were not allowed to call it 'war.' Linguistic regulations prescribed that, correctly speaking, it be called a 'surprise attack.' For which, strange to say, we were not in the least prepared. We did not know what we intended to do, and so we did not really try to learn the Greeks' intentions. I say 'we,' I started to say 'we' again many years ago. I accepted my parents back in misfortune. But at the time, when the Greek fleet rose against the horizon, a dreadful sight; when our hearts sank; when our young men went laughing to meet the enemy, into certain death, with no more protection than their leather shields; then I passionately cursed all those responsible. A defensive ring! An advance line behind a fortification! Trenches! There was nothing of the sort. True, I was no military strategist, but anyone could see how our soldiers were being herded toward the enemy along the level shore to be butchered. I have never been able to get that picture out of my mind.

And then, on the very first day, my brother Troilus.

I have always tried not to remember how he died, and yet nothing in the whole war left a keener imprint. Shortly I myself am to be slaughtered, and fear fear

fear forces me to think; yet even now I remember every cursed detail about my brother Troilus's death, and this one dead man would have lasted me the rest of the war. Proud, loyal to my king, daring, trusting in Hector's vow that no Greek would ever set foot on our shores, I stayed in the temple of Apollo outside the city, from which one used to look out on the coast. I just thought 'used to look out,' but it should be 'still looks out.' The temple has been spared. No Greek laid violent hands on Apollo's shrine. Whoever is standing there now looks out on the coast covered with debris, corpses, war material, which Troy once governed, and when he turns around he sees the destroyed city. Cybele, help.

Marpessa is sleeping. The children are sleeping.

Cybele, help.

That day saw the start of something that became a habit: I stood and saw. Went on standing when the other priests, including Panthous, had fled in panic toward Troy. When the uncompromising leather-cheeked old priestess Herophile fled into the interior of the temple in horror. I stood there. Saw how my brother Hector-Dim-Cloud – oh, he was wearing his leather jerkin! – smote the first Greeks who left the ships and waded through the shallow water, trying to reach the shores of Troy. My Trojans cut down the second wave of Greeks, too. Would Hector be proved right? I saw the human dolls fall to the ground, soundlessly and sufficiently far away. There was not the tiniest spark of triumph in my heart. Then indeed something quite different began; I saw it.

A formation of Greeks in close array, wearing armour and surrounding themselves with an unbroken wall of shields, stormed onto land like a single organism with a head and many limbs, while they set up a howl whose like had never been heard. Those on the outlying edges were quickly killed by the already exhausted Trojans, as no doubt it had been intended that they should be. Those toward the centre slew altogether too many of our men. The core reached shore as they were meant to, and with them the core's core: the Greek hero Achilles. He was intended to get through even if all the others fell. He did get through. 'So that's how it's done,' I heard myself tell myself feverishly. 'All for one.' What now? Cunningly he did not attack Hector, whom the other Greeks took in charge. He went for the boy Troilus, who was driven toward him by well-trained men the way game is driven toward the hunter. So that's how it's done. My heart began to pound. Troilus stood his ground, faced his opponent, fought. He fought by the rules, as he had been taught was the way to fight between high-born men. He adhered faithfully to the rules of the athletic contests in which he had excelled since childhood. Troilus! I was trembling. I knew ahead of time each step he would take, each turn of his head, each design he would trace with his body. But Achilles. Achilles the brute did not respond to the boy's offer.

Perhaps he did not understand it. Achilles raised his sword high above his head, gripping it with both hands, and let it whistle down on my brother. All rules fell into the dust for ever. So that's how it's done.

My brother Troilus fell to the ground. Achilles the brute was on top of him. I refused to believe it, I believed it at once. I was at odds with myself as so often in the past. If I saw what I think I saw, he strangled my brother as he lay. Something happened that went beyond my conception, beyond the conception of us all. Those who could see saw it the first day: we would lose this war. This time I did not shriek. Did not go crazy. Went on standing there. Broke the clay goblet in my hand without noticing.

The worst was still to come, is still to come. Troilus, wearing light armour, had gotten up again, had wrenched himself free from Achilles' hands, began to run – ye gods, how he could run! Aimlessly at first; then – I signalled, shouted – he found the direction, ran toward me, ran to the temple. Saved. We would lose the war but this brother, who at that moment seemed the dearest of them all, was saved. I ran to him, grabbed his arm, drew him into the interior of the temple – his throat was rattling, he was collapsing – in front of the god's statue, where he was safe. The repulsed Achilles wheezed after him; I no longer needed to pay him any notice. What I needed to do was to unfasten my brother's helmet, loosen his cuirass; he was gasping for air.

The old priestess Herophile, whom I never saw weep before or since, helped me. My hands flew. He who lives is not lost. Not lost to me, either. I will take care of you, Brother, I will love you, get to know you at last. 'Briseis will be happy,' I said into his ear.

Then Achilles the brute came. The murderer came into the temple, which darkened as he stood at the entrance. What did this man want? What was he after, wearing weapons here in the temple? Hideous moment: already I knew. Then he laughed. Every hair on my head stood on end and sheer terror came into my brother's eyes. I threw myself over him and was shoved aside as if I were not there. In what role was his enemy approaching my brother? As a murderer? As a seducer? Could such a thing be – the voluptuousness of the murderer and the lover in one? Was that allowed to exist among human beings? The fixed gaze of the victim. The capering approach of the pursuer, whom I now saw from behind, a lewd beast. Who took Troilus by the shoulders, stroked him, handled him – the defenceless boy from whom I, wretched woman, had removed the armour! Laughing, laughing all over. Gripped his neck. Moved to the throat. His plump, stubby-fingered, hairy hand on my brother's throat. Pressing, pressing. I hung on the murderer's arm, on which the veins stood out like cords. My brother's eyes were starting out of their sockets. And the gratification in Achilles' face. The naked hideous male gratification. If that exists, everything is possible.

It was deathly still. I was shaken off, felt nothing. Now the enemy, the monster, raised his sword in full view of Apollo's statue and severed my brother's head from his torso. Human blood spurted onto the altar as before it had spurted from the carcasses of our sacrificial animals. Troilus, the sacrificial victim. The butcher fled with a horrid and gratified howl. Achilles the brute. I felt nothing for a long time.

Then the touch. A hand on my cheek, which for the first time in my life seemed to be where it belonged. And a look I knew. Aeneas.

Everything in the past was pale premonition, uncompleted longing. Aeneas was the reality; and faithful to reality, craving reality, I wanted to cling to it. At the moment he could do nothing here, he said. He said he was leaving. 'Leave,' I said. Oh, how good he was at disappearing. I did not call after him, did not follow him, and did not try to find out about him. People said he was in the mountains. Many made faces of contempt. I did not defend him. Did not talk about him. Was with him with every fibre of my body and soul. Am with him. Aeneas. Live. You are my reserve force, I will not give you up. At the end you did not understand me, you threw the snake ring into the sea in anger. But we have not gotten to that point yet. The conversation with you comes later. When I need it. Yes, I will need it.

I insisted on being heard in the council as a witness to the death of Troilus. I demanded that this war be

ended at once. 'And how?' the men asked me, aghast.
I said. 'By telling the truth about Helen. By making
them offerings. Gold and other goods, whatever they
want. As long as they go away. As long as the
pestilential breath of their presence departs. By
admitting to what they will demand we admit – that
Paris gravely violated the right of hospitality, which
is sacred to us all, when he abducted Helen. The
Greeks must regard this action as a grievous rapine
and a grievous breach of trust. So they tell their wives,
their children, their slaves tales of what Paris did.
And they are right. End this war.'

Stalwart men turned pale as death. 'She's mad,' I
heard them whisper. 'Now she's mad.' And King
Priam, my father, rose slowly, dauntingly, to his feet
and then roared as no one ever heard him roar. His
daughter! Why must it be she of all people who spoke
for the enemy here in the council of Troy? Why did
she not speak for Troy instead: unequivocally,
publicly and loudly, here, in the temple and in the
marketplace? 'I was speaking for Troy, Father,' I
still ventured to say softly. I could not keep from
trembling. The king shook his fists, screamed: had I
forgotten so quickly the death of my brother Troilus!
'Throw that person out! She is no longer my child.'
The hands again, the smell of fear. I was led away.

Panthous told me that after I left the council discussed the oracle circulating through the streets of
Troy which said that Troy could win the war only if

Troilus reached twenty years old. Now, everyone knew that Troilus was seventeen when he fell. Calchas the seer, Calchas the traitor was behind the rumour, Eumelos claimed. 'So,' Panthous told me, 'I simply suggested that we pass a posthumous decree declaring Troilus to be twenty years old.' And Eumelos supplemented the suggestion: anyone who continued to maintain that Troilus was only seventeen when Achilles slew him would be punished. I said: 'I would be the first one you'd have to punish.' 'So what?' said Panthous. 'Why not, Cassandra?'

For the first time a chill came over me.

But King Priam put up a struggle. No (I was told he had said), insult his dead son further with lies? No. Not with his consent. So there was a time when the dead were sacred, at least to us; and I knew that time. The new time respected neither living nor dead. It took me a while to understand it. It was already inside the stronghold before the enemy came. It penetrated through every crack, how I do not know. Among us its name was Eumelos.

I was choosing the easy way out, Panthous the Greek instructed me. I had come to detest the way he used to hide behind impenetrable didacticism; but I was not inside his skin, the skin of a Greek. Once I asked him angrily whether he thought I was going to denounce him to Eumelos. 'How can I know that?' he asked, and smiled. 'Besides, what could you accuse me of?' We both knew that Eumelos made do without grounds. Of course he got Panthous years later, through the women. Blind, I was blind not to have seen the fear behind his game.

There is no more time left, and so self-reproach is not enough. I must ask myself what it was that made me blind. The humiliating thing is, I could have sworn I already had the answer, did have for a long time.

Should I get down out of the chariot, after all? The wickerwork where I am sitting is hard. One consolation: the willow rods that compose it grew by our river, the Scamander. Oenone took me there to gather willow wands, in the autumn after the war began. She said I should make them into a bed. 'They kill the desires,' Oenone said earnestly. 'Did Hecuba send you?' 'Arisbe,' she said. Arisbe. What did that woman know about me? She herself, Oenone said, had slept on willows all the months when Paris was away. She never spoke Aeneas's name. Absent-mindedly I listened to her disconsolate lament about Paris, who, she said, had been ruined by the foreign woman. What did Arisbe have in mind? Was she trying to warn me? To chastise me? I lay on the willows howling with rage. They did not help. I longed for love unbearably, a longing which only one man could appease; my dreams left no doubt about that. Once I took a very young priest into my bed. It was almost expected of me; I was training him and he revered me. I quenched his passion while I remained cold and dreamed of Aeneas. I began to pay heed to my body, which – who would have thought it! – obeyed the guidance of dreams.

It occurs to me that I had to do with willow wands twice more after that: the basket where I was imprisoned was wickerwork too, so densely woven that scarcely one ray of light got through to me. And later the women, I among them, laid suckling pigs on willow rods inside the caves, for Cybele. When I did that, I was free of the gods. Willow wands, my last seat. Without my realising it, my hand has begun to loosen a slender wand from the weave. It is broken but hardly moves. I will continue to tug and shake it, more attentively now. I want to set it free. I want to take it with me when the time comes that I must get down.

Now his wife is butchering Agamemnon.

Presently it will be my turn.

I notice that I cannot believe what I know.

That is how it always was, how it always will be.

I did not know it would be so difficult, not even when I realised with horror that we were going to disappear without a trace: Myrine, Aeneas, I. I told him that. He was silent. It comforted me that he had no comfort to offer. When we saw each other for the last time, he wanted to give me his ring, the snake ring. My eyes said no. He threw it from the cliff into the sea. The shining arc it described in the sunlight burned into my heart. No one will ever learn these all-important things about us. The scribes' tablets, baked in the flames of Troy, transmit the palace accounts, the records of grain, urns, weapons, prisoners. There are no signs for pain, happiness, love. That seems to me an extreme misfortune.

Marpessa is singing a song to the twins. She learned it, as I did, from her mother, Parthena the nurse. It says: 'When the child is sleeping, his soul, a beautiful bird, flies to the silver olive and then slowly mounts toward the setting sun.' Soul, beautiful bird. I felt its movements in my breast, sometimes light as a feather's touch, sometimes violent and painful. The war gripped the men's breasts and killed the bird. Only when it reached out for my soul too did I say no. A strange notion: the movements of the soul inside me resembled the movements of the children in my body, a gentle stirring, a motion like that in a dream. The first time I felt this frail dream-motion it shook me to the core, opened the barrier inside me which had held back my love for the children of a father who had been forced on me; the love rushed out with a river of tears. I looked at my children for the last time when the thickset Agamemnon, stomping over the red carpet, disappeared behind the door of the palace. Now I will not look at them again. Marpessa has covered them, hiding them from me.

You could say that it was through them, on their account, that I lost my father. Priam the king had three devices against a disobedient daughter. He could declare her insane. He could lock her up. He could force her into an unwanted marriage. This device, to be sure, was unprecedented. Never in Troy had the daughter of a free man been forced into marriage. This was the last extremity. My father sent for Eurypylos and his army of Mysians even though everyone knew that Eurypylos wanted me for his wife in exchange. When that happened it was clear to us all: Troy was lost. Now I, Hecuba the queen, the unhappy Polyxena, all my sisters, indeed all the women in Troy, were seized by ambivalence: they had to hate Troy even while they wished it the victory.

So many brothers, so much grief. So many sisters, so much horror. Oh, the dreadful fertility of Hecuba.

When I think of Troilus, Hector, Paris, my heart bleeds. When I think of Polyxena, I feel like flying into a rage. If only nothing survived me but my hatred. If the hatred sprouted from my grave, a tree of hate that would whisper: 'Achilles the brute.' If they felled the tree, it would grow again. If they pinned it down, each blade of grass would take over the message: 'Achilles the brute, Achilles the brute.' And every minstrel who dared to sing of Achilles would die in torture on the spot. Between the brute and posterity, let there be an abyss of contempt or oblivion. Apollo, if you do exist after all, grant me this; I would not have lived in vain.

I saw how those who fought on the battlefield gradually came to believe the lies of those who knew nothing of battle, because they flattered them. There is such an accord between the two that often I was tempted to despise human nature. The women in the mountains exorcised my arrogance. Not by words. By being different, by extracting from their nature qualities I hardly dared dream of. If I still have time, I should speak of my body.

After the death of Troilus, Briseis, daughter of Calchas, almost lost her mind. Many were the women I heard shriek in those years – but the shrieks of Briseis when we buried Troilus curdled our blood. For a long time she let no one speak to her and did not speak a word herself. Her first word was a soft 'yes' when I brought her the message from her father, Calchas. If the king would allow it, she wanted to go and join her renegade father on the other side. I had the impression that the king was only too glad to grant her request without delay. Obviously a daughter in mourning belonged with her father who loved her, he said. King Priam, I thought, was not sorry to see the last of a woman who mourned as she did. I had already heard whispers in the palace that her grief was undermining morale. Eumelos, to be sure, was indignant. 'What?' he asked insidiously. Did the king consider blood ties more important than those of the state? 'Indeed I do,' said Priam; he was the old Priam and I loved him. How could I not? And the fact that he cursed me in the council – didn't that show how attached he was to me? No. It would take more than that to make me disown my father, good King Priam.

As Briseis's friend, I accompanied her to the Greek camp; that too seemed reasonable to everyone except Eumelos. With us came two of my brothers and five warriors, all unarmed. Not one of us Trojans doubted that a Trojan woman who is going to her father deserves a worthy escort. But the Greeks seemed confused by us, almost anxious! Calchas, after he had greeted his daughter tenderly and warily, explained our strange reception. 'Never,' he said, 'would one of the Greeks enter the enemy camp unarmed.' 'But they would have our word that they would be safe if they did that,' I cried. Calchas the seer smiled. 'A word! Adapt, Cassandra. The sooner the better. If I had not terrified them, they would have done in your unarmed brothers.' 'Terrified them, how?' 'By telling them about the magical power one of our unarmed warriors possesses, especially when he is accompanied by a woman.' 'One of our warriors, Calchas?' 'One of us Trojans, Cassandra.' For the first time in my life I saw a man gutted by home-sickness.

We were standing by the sea, the waves were licking our feet. I saw the heaps of weapons – spears, javelins, swords, shields – behind the wooden wall which the Greeks had swiftly erected against us along the coast. Calchas understood my gaze, replied: 'You are lost.' I wanted to test him. 'We could give Helen back to Menelaus,' I said. Again he smiled his painful smile: 'Could you really?'

A shock: he knew. Did they all know then, all the men who were swaggering up to gape at me and Briseis: the temperate Menelaus, the keenly observant Odysseus. Agamemnon, whom I instantly disliked? Diomedes of Argos, a lanky fellow. They stood and stared. 'In Troy men don't look at women that way,' I said in our language, which only Calchas could understand. 'They certainly don't,' he replied unmoved. 'Get used to it.' 'And this is where you are taking Briseis? To these men?' 'She must live,' said Calchas. 'Survive. Nothing more. Life at any cost.'

So now I knew why Calchas was with the Greeks.

No, Calchas, I said. At any cost? Not so.

Today I think differently. I was so calm. Now everything inside me is in revolt. I will beg that terrible woman for my life. I will throw myself at her feet. 'Clytemnestra, lock me up for ever in your darkest dungeon. Give me barely enough to live on. But I implore you: send me a scribe, or better yet a young slave woman with a keen memory and a powerful voice. Ordain that she may repeat to her daughter what she hears from me. That the daughter in turn may pass it on to her daughter, and so on. So that alongside the river of heroic songs this tiny rivulet, too, may reach those faraway, perhaps happier people who will live in times to come.'

And could I believe that, even for one day?

Slay me, Clytemnestra. Kill me. Hurry.

Inside the citadel they are drinking. The wanton

clamour I would so gladly not have heard is rising to a crescendo now. So on top of everything else the men who come to fetch me will be drunk.

We did not see the hero Achilles when we delivered Briseis to her fate. He was her fate. He saw us from some hidden place. How my heart burned when I embraced her. With an unmoved face she stood leaning against Diomedes, whom she had just seen for the first time in her life. The ungainly lout. I pictured my delicate boyish brother Troilus. 'Briseis!' I said softly, 'what are you thinking of?' 'He loves me,' she replied. 'He says he loves me.' I saw him place his hand on her the way men touch slave women. The Greek men all around us laughed their booming male laughs. I was seized by a ghastly fear of the love of the Greeks.

But where was Achilles? His name was boring into me; when I mentioned it, I saw Calchas lose his look of composure at last. The mask cracked. Before me stood the Trojan I knew, the friend of my early child-hood, my father's shrewd, temperate adviser. He drew me aside, paid no heed to the suspicion of the Greeks, which he aroused when he evidently confided to me a secret that was weighing on his mind. Yes, Achilles. He was a problem to Calchas, too. Achilles and the Greeks (he said) claimed that Achilles was the son of a goddess. Her name: Thetis. Well. We priests decided among ourselves not to form an opinion. Achilles gave away many weapons and much wine to ensure

the spread of the legend. He threatened the grimmest
punishment to anyone who dared to doubt its truth –
and no doubt about it, that man had not his equal in
meting out punishment. So, Calchas said, what he
told me now could easily cost him his life. Namely:
when the war was about to begin, Odysseus and
Menelaus were assembling the Greek allies (he,
Calchas, had been present at the negotiations and
since then he had known what it meant to be a
Greek); then they came to fetch Achilles, too. His
mother, goddess or not, said that he was not at home,
that he was far away, that he had left on a journey.
Odysseus, who knows people and up to a certain point
himself as well (which is rare) – Odysseus smelled a
rat. He left the rat and Menelaus (whom all the Greeks
secretly despised because he had lost Helen) with the
woman, followed his keen nose, and found Achilles
in a secluded room, in bed with another young man.
And since the practised, far-seeing Odysseus had tried
to evade the levy himself by pretending to be mad
(What, we didn't know that? Well, what *did* we know
about our enemies, then?); since he would not allow
another man to get off when he had to bleed, he
literally dragged Achilles into the war by the scruff
of his neck. It might be that he already regretted it.
For Achilles was after everyone in sight: young men,
whom he genuinely desired, and girls, as a proof that
he was like everybody else. A fiend in battle so that
everyone would see he was not a coward, he did not

know what to do with himself once the fighting was done. And this was the man to whom Calchas the seer later had to turn over his daughter. Perhaps he fooled himself into thinking that among wanton men, only the most wanton could protect a woman. I saw Briseis again after the fall of Troy, when we were driven through the camp of the Greeks. I thought I had seen all the horror a human being can see. I know what I am saying: Briseis's face surpassed it all.

If only he, Achilles, had died a thousand deaths. If only I could have been present at every one.

Let the earth vomit out his ashes.

I am very tired.

On that long-ago day when we returned from the Greek camp without Briseis, I felt I had been away for a long time and very, very far. There lay my Troy, my beloved city, behind its high wall. The target, the prey. A god had given me new eyes. Suddenly I saw all the weaknesses which the Greeks could exploit. I swore to myself that never, never should a man like Achilles walk through our streets. Except for this last day of all, I was never more of a Trojan than that day. I saw that the others were feeling the same thing I did. So we came home, to the Scaean Gate. There the sentries intercepted us. We were shown into a small, dark, stinking room in the gatehouse. Eumelos's men dictated our names to an embarrassed, pompous scribe. All of us had to say who we were, even my brothers and I, whom everyone knew. I burst out laughing, was severely reprimanded. Where had we been, we were asked. 'So, with the enemy. And for what purpose?'

Then I thought I was dreaming. The men were searched – even my brothers, the king's sons – pocket by pocket, seam by seam. I held the bright knife to the chest of the first man who touched me, the knife I carried on me for all eventualities, so as not to be at the mercy of the enemy. 'I didn't need it over *there*,' I said bitterly.

What did I mean by that, I was asked. Was I comparing a Trojan loyal to his king to the enemy? I knew the man who dared to speak this way to me: physically gone to pot, bloated, running to fat. He had tried to touch me in the past. I ruminated and said coldly: 'Anyone who touches me will end up with a knife in him.' The man retreated, half grovelling, like a dog. Oh yes, I knew him. My father's chief scribe. Was he one of Eumelos's men? What was happening to my city, then? What was happening to my Trojans that they did not see our little band being driven through their streets? It was simple, I saw: simply not to see. I could not find their eyes. Coldly I scrutinised the backs of their heads. Had they always been so cowardly? Was there such a thing as a people who had cowardly backs of heads? I asked Eumelos, who, seemingly by chance, was waiting for us at the entrance of the palace. I got under his skin. He hectored his deputy: 'But not her! One must be able to draw distinctions. Not everyone who knew Briseis the traitor, or even was her friend, is under our suspicion. But what if what Cassandra calls cowardly (exaggerating as we know she is in the habit of doing) is simply loyalty to the king? It goes without saying that you are all free.'

Priam explained to me that in war everything that would apply in peace was rescinded. After all, it did not hurt Briseis what people said about her here, where she would never return. And it was helping us. 'In what way?' 'Inasmuch as opinions about her case differed.' 'In heaven's name, how can opinions differ about a case that does not exist? That was invented especially for the purpose?' 'Even if that's true, once something has become public knowledge, it is real.' 'So. Real like Helen.'

Then he threw me out for the second time. Things were beginning to add up; was I addled or something? I think so. I think in a certain sense I was. I lived through it, but it is still hard to explain it to myself. I still believed that a little will to truth, a little courage, could erase the whole misunderstanding. To call what was true, true and what was untrue, false: that was asking so little (I thought) and would have served our cause better than any lie or half-truth. For it was intolerable (I thought) to base the whole war – and our whole lives, for wasn't war our life! – on the accident of a lie. It was out of the question (I thought, although I can hardly recall it) that the rich plenty of our existence should be reduced to one pigheaded contention. After all, we need only call to mind our Trojan tradition. But what was that tradition? What did it consist in? Then I understood: in the Helen we had invented, we were defending everything that we no longer had. And the more it faded, the more real we had to say it was. Thus out of words, gestures, ceremonies, and silence there arose a second Troy, a ghostly city, where we were supposed to feel at home and live at ease. Was I the only one who saw this? Feverishly I checked the names. My father. I could no longer speak to him. My mother, who closed herself off more and more. Arisbe. Parthena the nurse. You, Marpessa. Then something, a secret fear, warned me not to look into your world before I was ready. Better to suffer but to remain where I was. Where my brothers and sisters moved about without question, as if there were solid ground beneath their feet. Where Herophile, the old leather-cheeked priestess, fervently dedicated offerings to the god Apollo, beseeching him to support our arms. Impossible that the king's daughter and a priestess should doubt the royal family and have faith in her servant girl and her nurse. You all stepped like shadows, Marpessa, to the edge of my field of vision. You became shadows. Deprived of reality. As I myself became unreal, the more I treated as real what the palace of Eumelos commanded. The palace's greatest ally in winning my allegiance was our best enemy, Achilles.

My attention, everyone's attention, focused on the monstrous crimes of this rabid beast, who with his wanton band had thrown himself on the countryside around Mount Ida – where Aeneas was! He plundered the villages, massacred the men, raped the women, cut the throats of the goats and sheep, trampled down the fields. Aeneas! I trembled with fear. One month later he entered the stronghold leading those Dardanians who had managed to save themselves. Everyone was yelling and weeping; it was my most beautiful day ever. It was always like that when he and I breathed the same air; life flowed back into the husk of my body. When I stood on the wall at evening I saw the sun again, the moon and stars; the olive trees flashing silver in the wind; the purple, metallic sheen of the sea at sunset; the shifting brown and blue tones of the plain. The fragrance of the thyme fields wafted over to me; I felt how soft the air was. Aeneas was alive. I did not have to see him, I could wait until he came to me. He was towed off to the council; there was a lively, almost cheerful bustle in the streets of Troy. A saying made the rounds, no one claimed to have invented it and everyone seemed to know it at the same moment: 'If Hector is our arm, Aeneas is the soul of Troy.' Thank-fires burned at all the sacrificial shrines in his honour. 'But that's preposterous!' I heard him say to Herophile, our high priestess. 'Are you thanking the gods for letting our land be devastated?' 'We're giving thanks for your rescue, Aeneas,' she said. 'Nonsense. My rescue was a by-product of the enemy's devastation.' 'Should we extinguish the sacrificial fires? Make the gods even more angry?' 'As far as I'm concerned, yes.' I saw Aeneas leave the temple. The quarrel went unnoticed. The sacrifices proceeded; I helped perform the rituals as my office required: passes, gestures, words without meaning. At night Aeneas stayed in the humble accommodations assigned to the fugitives. I lay awake, tortured myself wondering whether he equated me with Herophile, the stubborn old high priestess. For my benefit – and his – I compiled the differences. To my amazement I found there was not much to choose between us for anyone looking on from the outside. The difference I took such pride in amounted to nothing more than my inner reservations. This was not enough to satisfy him, Aeneas. Was it enough for me?

After a long, desolate spell without dreams, I finally had another dream one night. It was one of those dreams which I realised at once was significant, which I did not understand immediately but did not forget. I was walking alone through a strange city; it was not Troy, but Troy was the only city I had ever seen before. My dream city was larger, more extensive. I knew it was night, yet the moon and the sun were in the sky at the same time and were struggling for dominance. I had been appointed judge (by whom it was not stated): which of the two heavenly bodies could shine more brightly? There was something wrong about this contest, but try as I might, I could not find out what. Until finally, disheartened and anxious, I said that of course everyone knew and could see that it was the sun that shone most brightly. 'Phoebus Apollo!' a voice cried in triumph, and at the same time, to my horror, Selene, the dear lady of the moon, sank to the horizon lamenting. A judgment had been passed on me; but how could I be guilty when I had done nothing but tell the truth?

Posing this question, I woke up. I told Marpessa my dream, casually and with artificial laughter. She said nothing. For many days she kept her face averted. Then she came, showed me her eyes, which it seemed to me had grown darker and deeper, and said: 'The most important thing about your dream, Cassandra, was that faced with a completely perverted question, you nevertheless tried to find an answer. You should remember that when the time comes.'

'Who says so? To whom did you tell my dream?'

'Arisbe,' Marpessa replied, as if it were obvious, and I was silent. Had I secretly hoped to have my dream referred to her, to Arisbe? Did that mean she had authority over my dreams? I knew that the answer was already in the questions, and I felt a stirring inside me after the long freeze brought on by the first months of the war. Already spring was coming again; the Greeks had not attacked us for a long time; I left the fortress, sat on a hill above the Scamander River. What did that mean: the sun shone brighter than the moon?

Was the moon ever intended to shine brighter? Who put such questions into my head? If I understood Arisbe rightly, I was entitled – perhaps even obligated – to reject them. One coil in the rope that bound me, the outermost coil, snapped, dropped away; many others remained. It was a time to draw breath, to stretch stiff joints; a blossoming of the flesh.

At the new moon Aeneas came. Strange that Marpessa was not sleeping in the anteroom as was her duty. I saw his face for only a moment as he blew out the light that swam in a pool of oil beside the door. Our recognition sign was and remained his hand on my cheek, my cheek in his hand. We said little more to each other than our names; I had never heard a more beautiful love poem. Aeneas Cassandra. Cassandra Aeneas. When my chastity encountered his shyness, our bodies went wild. I could not have dreamed what my limbs replied to the questions of his lips, or what unknown inclinations his scent would confer on me. And what a voice my throat had at its command.

But Troy's soul was destined not to stay in Troy. Very early the next morning he boarded ship with a troop of armed men; he had to put up a fight to be allowed to take his own men, the Dardanians. This was the last ship for a long time to carry goods to the coasts of the Black Sea. I believe – and I understood him yet failed to understand – that Aeneas preferred to leave rather than to stay. Admittedly, it was hard to think of him and Eumelos sitting at the same table. Stick with his father, he enjoined me. For months on end he vanished from my sight. Time seemed to slow down; in my memory it was pale and ghostly, punctuated only by the great rituals I had to help perform, and by the public oracles to which our people flocked for desperately needed comfort. My brother Helenus and Laocoön, priest of Poseidon, an estimable man, were their favourite oracles; but I could not help seeing that they were spreading empty chatter. Helenus, surprised by my indignation, did not dispute that the oracles were more or less made to order. Made to whose order? Well, the royal family's, the temple's; what was the matter with me? That was the way it had always been, for the oracles were the mouths of those who appointed them and who were divine almost as the gods themselves were divine. How rare it was that a god condescended to speak through us; after all, I must know that better than anyone. And yet how often we required the gods' counsel. So who got hurt if he, Helenus, prophesied that the Greeks would never conquer our city unless through the weakest gate, the Scaean Gate? Besides, he himself believed this was true, subjectively speaking; and it achieved the highly desirable effect of increasing the alertness of the sentries at the Scaean Gate still further. Or take Laocoön. Laocoön (he said) divined, from the entrails of the last sacrificial bull, that Troy would be threatened only if ten of the twelve white horses in our royal stables fell into the hands of the Greeks. It was unthinkable that that should occur. Yet now, as a result of the prophecy, the right interior flank of the stronghold where the stables lay was also especially secure. What in the world could I have against that?

Nothing: that was all I could say. How can I explain? Helenus was careless but not a fraud. Exactly my age, handsome, I always liked to behave condescendingly to him: my superior. What made him superior? His faith, no doubt about it. In the gods? No. His faith that we were in the right, and doubly in the right if we forced the word of the gods to come down to us. He acted and spoke in good faith, in the faith that the world was exactly as he proclaimed it. No one could inflict doubt on him; never did I see on his face so much as a shadow of that smile which by now had engraved itself into the corners of Panthous's mouth. He accepted his popularity in the way that people like: casually, as something that he had coming to him, and without placing unnecessary burdens on them or himself. He got along remarkably well with Hector and one day made the surprising prediction that Hector would carry the fame of Troy through all time to come. Andromache – Hector's wife since the beginning of the war, loyal, domestic, rather plain – was crying her eyes out. She came running to tell me her dreams; people had gotten into the habit of doing that. Hector dreamed (Andromache told me) that he was pushed out of the warm womb of a bitch, through a dreadful narrow opening, and into the world, where he was forced to change at once from a sheltered and cherished puppy into a ravening boar. The boar accosts a lion and – in the scorching sun! – is overwhelmed and torn to shreds. Her husband woke up bathed in tears, Andromache confided. He was not the kind of man heroes are made of, she said. In the gods' name, would I entreat Hecuba on his behalf: everyone knew he was her favourite son.

What a child my eldest brother was. I was angry at Hecuba for having coddled him and kept him a little boy, and I thought it right and proper that she should intervene on his behalf. To my great astonishment Anchises, Aeneas's much-loved father, was conferring with her. No doubt of it, Hecuba, my mother, had appointed him to comfort her because she could do nothing, nothing whatever for Hector; they were grooming him for the role of Chief Hero. Hector-Dim-Cloud! A number of my brothers were better suited than he to lead the battle. But Eumelos wanted to strike at the queen through her favourite son. If he failed as a hero, he and along with him his mother would become the laughingstock of the city. If he did as he was asked and led the battle, he would be killed sooner or later. Cursed Eumelos. Hecuba looked at me and said: 'Cursed war.' All three of us were silent. I learned that protest begins with this silence in which more than one takes part.

Anchises. If only Anchises were here. If he were with me I could bear anything. He did not allow you to fear that anything could be unbearable, no matter what happened. Yes, the unbearable did exist. But why fear it long before it arrives! Why not simply live, and if possible cheerfully? Cheerfulness, that is the word for him. Gradually I saw where he got it from: he saw through people, above all himself, but he did not feel disgusted by what he saw like Panthous; he enjoyed it. Anchises was – no, is – a free man. He thinks dispassionately even about people who wish him ill. Eumelos, for example. It would never have occurred to me to talk about Eumelos gaily and without prejudice. To understand and feel compassion for him rather than to fear and hate him. 'Just consider the fact that he has no wife,' Anchises said. 'Y–e–e–s – you women don't suspect what that means to a man. That he has to force slave women to sleep with him. That he can smell you gloating. Oh yes, a man like that can smell what's going on around him. After all, he's after the same thing as the rest of us, he only wants to get back to where he had it good once: under your skirts. You won't let him in. So he takes revenge, it's as simple as that. A bit of responsiveness from your lot and who knows, he might be cured.'

How we tore into him. So evil was a deficiency? An illness? Something that could be cured? 'Well,' he admitted then, 'maybe for Eumelos there's no more hope.' Nevertheless, he still maintained: 'That man is

a product of Troy just like – let's say like King Priam.'
Anchises used to plead the most monstrous things
with a laugh, but here he was going too far. Eumelos
was an aberration, I cried, a sort of accident, an over-
sight of the gods if there was such a thing. If there was
such a thing as gods. Whereas Priam . . . 'Whereas
Priam does nothing more than appoint Eumelos to
office,' Anchises said dryly. 'Is that right? Another
aberration?' 'Of course.' 'So, an accident?'

What could I say to that? Oh, how I resisted
admitting that Priam and Eumelos were a matched
pair who needed each other. For weeks I avoided
Anchises, until the incredible happened. The palace
guard barred Hecuba the queen from taking part in
the sessions of the council. Now (I thought when I
heard), now order in the palace is collapsing; and I
actually felt amazed that I was looking forward with
joy as well as anxiety to the change that now was
bound to occur. Nothing happened. They did not
look at her, my mother Hecuba reported in Anchises's
hut, where I arrived out of breath from running.
None of the men had looked at her when they walked
past her into the council. 'Not even my son Hector,'
Hecuba said bitterly. 'I stepped into his way. Eyed
him from top to toe – well, you both know how I can
look. "Try to understand, Mother," he said. "We
want to spare you. The things we have to talk about
in our council, now in wartime, are no longer the
concern of women." '

'Quite right,' said Anchises. 'Now they are the concern of children.'

Now Hecuba the queen discussed with him everything that weighed on her mind. I did not feel comfortable to see such intimacy between my mother and Aeneas's father. But I conceded to her that Anchises made everything easier. He admired Hecuba; you could see he would have admired her no less if she had not been the king's wife. He treated me like a very dear and respected daughter; but he did not talk about his son Aeneas before I spoke of him myself. His tact was as inalienable as his good cheer. He expressed his feelings not only with his mobile face but with the whole of his high, bald skull. Oenone, who loved him like a father, used to say: 'His mouth is laughing, but his forehead is sad.' You could not help but look at his hands, which were almost always working a piece of wood, or at least feeling it, while his eyes might suddenly listen to find out what quality or form was hidden in the wood. He never had a tree chopped down without first conferring with it at length; without first removing from it a seed or a twig which he could plant in the earth to ensure its continued existence. He knew everything there was to know about wood and trees. And the figures he carved when we sat around together, he then gave away like a prize; they became a sign by which we could recognise each other. If you entered a house and found one of Anchises's carvings, animal or human, you knew you could speak openly, that you could ask for help in any matter, no matter how critical. When the Greeks were massacring all the Amazons, we hid Myrine and a number of her sisters in huts whose anteroom contained a small wooden calf, goat, or pig made by Anchises. Wordlessly the women would draw them over to the fire, throw a piece of clothing over them, blacken their cheeks, press a spindle or a spoon into their hands which knew nothing of women's work, even take the youngest child from the bed and place it in the lap of the harried foreign woman. Not once were we disappointed by a family to whom Anchises gave a carved figure. He knew people. And his hut under the fig tree outside the Dardanian Gate was visited only by people who suited him. Otherwise he would talk with everyone, he did not turn away anyone who wanted to visit him. He welcomed even Andron, the young officer who worked for Eumelos and who had us searched after we had delivered Briseis. That went against my grain very much: for what if Hecuba should run into this man here, where she often came in order to spare Anchises from having to come to her in the palace; what if Oenone, Parthena the nurse, Marpessa, or even Arisbe should meet him! 'Why not?' Anchises said, unmoved. 'Better here than somewhere else. Go ahead and talk to him. What does it cost you? One shouldn't give up on anyone until he's dead.' I felt ashamed without being able to agree with him. As far as I could see, he had no dealings with the gods. But he believed in people. When it came to that, he was younger than all of us. It was at his place, under the changing foliage of the giant fig tree, that we began to live our life of freedom; in the middle of the war, completely unprotected, surrounded by an ever-growing horde of people armed to the teeth. Meanwhile, the internal order of the palace, which I had taken for eternal, was changing before my unbelieving eyes the way woodchips, straw, and grass floating on a river are carried along by the stronger current. The stronger current was the king's party, to which I, his daughter, did not belong. Instead, it was composed of younger men who went around in groups, expressed their views loudly when they met, continually felt they were under attack, believed they had to defend themselves against reproaches which had never been voiced, and found officious men – bards, scribes – who supplied them phrases for their punctilious affectations. 'To save face' was one such phrase. 'To show no reaction' was another. Anchises shook with laughter. 'Whatever does that mean!' he cried. 'As if people could *not* save their faces! Or are they telling us, without realising it, that the faces they customarily show to the world are not their own? Simpletons.'

Indeed, Anchises made everything easier. For it was not easy for me to leave the domain of the fig tree, at least that is how it seemed to me. Part of me – the gay, friendly, unconstrained part – stayed behind, outside the citadel, with 'them.' I used to say 'they' when I referred to the people in Anchises's circle, not 'we'; I was not yet allowed to say 'we.' Vacillating and fragile and amorphous was the 'we' I used, went on using as long as I possibly could. It included my father, but did it any longer include me? Yet for me there was no Troy without King Priam my father. Each evening that part of me which was loyal to the king, obedient, obsessed with conformity, returned to the fortress with a heavy heart. The 'we' that I clung to grew transparent, feeble, more and more unprepossessing, and consequently I was more and more out of touch with my 'I.' Yet other people knew perfectly well who I was, they had established my identity, to them it was clear: I was a prophetess and interpreter of dreams. An authority figure. When their future prospects looked bleak, when their own help-lessness afflicted them, they came to me. My dear sister Polyxena had been the first; she was followed by her women friends and by her friends' friends. All Troy was dreaming and referring its dreams to me.

Yes. Yes. Yes. Now I will have a talk with myself about Polyxena. About the guilt which cannot be extinguished, not if Clytemnestra were to murder me twenty times over. Polyxena was the last name spoken between Aeneas and me, the occasion of our last (perhaps our only) misunderstanding. He believed that it was on her account that I could not leave with him, and he tried to convince me that I could not help my dead sister by staying. But I knew that, if I knew anything. We did not have time to finish talking about my refusal to go with him, which had to do not with the past but with the future. Aeneas is alive. He will learn of my death. If he is the same man I love, he will continue to wonder why I chose captivity and death rather than him. Perhaps he will understand even without my help what it was that I had to reject at the cost of my life: submission to a role contrary to my nature.

Evasion, digression, those are always my tactics when her name comes up for discussion: Polyxena. She was the other woman. She was the woman I could not be. She had everything I lacked. Of course I know they called me 'beautiful,' even 'the most beautiful,' but their faces remained solemn when they said it. When she passed by they all smiled, the highest-ranking priest as well as the humblest slave, the most dim-witted kitchen maid. I search for a word to describe her; I cannot help that; my belief that a successful phrase – words, that is – can capture or even produce every phenomenon and every event, will outlive me. But where she is concerned I fail. She was composed of many elements, of charm and meltingness; and of firmness, even hardness. There was a contradiction in her nature that was both maddening and attractive. You wanted to seize it, protect it, or rip it out of her even if you had to destroy her in order to do it. She had many friends whom she did not hold at arm's length, from social strata I did not mix with at that time; she used to sing with them, songs she made up herself. She was kind and at the same time had the evil eye, with which she could see inside me but not inside herself. Yes. It took self-denial for me to accept her, she did not meet me halfway. Since I became priestess, since the year she did not speak to me, we dealt with each other as the custom of the palace required of sisters. But we both knew that we could not avoid a clash, and each of us knew that the other knew.

So I was shocked when she, Polyxena of all people, came to tell me her dreams. And what dreams! Insoluble tangles. And I, I of all people, was supposed to tell her what they meant. She could only hate me after that, and in fact this is what she seemed to want. She delivered herself into my hands with an unbridled, inquiring, and dreaming gaze. She dreamed that she was in a garbage pit and stretched out her arms toward a radiant figure for whom she was consumed with passion. Who was the lucky man, I asked, trying to joke. Did he have a name? Polyxena said dryly, 'Yes. It's Andron.'

Andron. Eumelos's officer. Words failed me. My accursed office. 'Yes,' I said. 'The things people dream, you know. You dream of the last person you saw that day. It doesn't mean anything, Polyxena.' I did not say anything about the garbage pit. Neither did she.

She went away disappointed. Came again. In her dream she had coupled in the most degrading way with Andron, Eumelos's officer, whom she hated while she was awake. So she said. So what was wrong with her? 'Hey, Sister,' I said as hoydenishly as I could, 'I believe you need a man.' 'I have one,' she said. 'He gives me nothing.' She was agonised. Hatefully, as if she was able to take revenge on me at last, she demanded that I tell her what she could not tell herself: that something alien inside her was forcing her to burn with passion for this puffed-up young cub. For this nonentity of a man who had no other way of getting people to talk about him than by entering the dishonourable service of Eumelos. She abhorred him, she said. I cannot say that I was any help to her in the beginning. Instead of loosening the knot that constricted her, I pulled it tighter by my incomprehension. I did not want to know why my sister Polyxena could feel the deepest gratification only by getting down in the dirt and submitting to the unworthiest of men. I could not help the contempt I felt at Polyxena's dreams; of course she sensed this and could not stand it. She began a relationship with Andron in secret. That was unheard-of. Never had any of us sisters had to conceal her amorous inclinations. Incredulous and deeply uneasy, I watched the underside of life in the palace reveal itself, as if it were being turned to disclose a lewd grimace. I watched how its balance overturned as its centre shifted. Polyxena was one of the victims the palace buried beneath it.

What I did not understand then, and did not want to understand, was that many were prepared to be victims, not only from the outside, but through something in themselves. Everything in me revolted against that. Why?

Now all of a sudden it is truly still. I am infinitely grateful for the stillness before death. For this moment that fills me completely so that I do not have to think anything. For this bird who flies soundlessly and far away across the sky, transforming it almost imperceptibly. But my eye, which knows the look of all the skies, cannot be deceived. Evening is coming on.

Time is running out. What else do I have to know?

I could not help despising Polyxena because I did not want to despise myself. That cannot be, but I know that is how it is. Why do I go on living if not to learn the things one learns before death? I believe Polyxena perished in a way that was fearful beyond measure, because not she but I was the king's favourite daughter. She perished because I based my life on that tenet for far too long. Because I insisted on its truth. Refused to let it be impugned. To whom else did she confide her secret besides me, her sister; me, the seeress? What use to her, what use to me, to repeat now the phrase I came up with at the time, in my infirmity: 'I am only human, too.' What is that supposed to mean, 'too'? I was overtaxed, that is true. She, Polyxena, expected too much of me, because too much had been expected of her. In short, while she was sleeping with Andron she began to dream about King Priam. Seldom at first but always the same thing; then more often, in the end every night. It was more than she could bear. In her distress she came back to me again, after all. Her father violated her in her dream, she said. She was weeping. No one can answer for his dreams, but one can keep them to oneself. That is what I gave my sister to understand. I believe I was trembling with indignation. Polyxena broke down. I took care of her and made sure that she kept silent. At this time I could not receive Aeneas and he did not come on his own, either. I stopped visiting Anchises. In my entrails sat an animal that gnawed at me and preyed on my mind. Later I learned its name: panic. I found rest only in the temple precincts.

I immersed myself in the ceremonial with seeming fervour, perfected my techniques as a priestess, taught the young priestesses the difficult skill of speaking in chorus, enjoyed the solemn atmosphere on the high feast days, the detachment of the priests from the mass of the faithful, my guiding role in the great pageant; the pious awe and admiration in the looks of the common people; the superiority my office conferred on me. I needed to be present and at the same time unaffected. For by that time I had stopped believing in the gods.

No one noticed that except Panthous, who used to observe me. I could not say for how long I had been an unbeliever. If I had had some shock, an experience resembling conversion, I could remember. But faith ebbed away from me gradually, the way illnesses sometimes ebb away, and one day you tell yourself that you are well. The illness no longer finds any foothold in you. That is how it was with my faith. What foothold could it still have found in me? Two occur to me: first hope, then fear. Hope had left me. I still knew fear, but fear alone does not know the gods; they are very vain, they want to be loved too, and hopeless people do not love them. At that time my aspect began to change. Aeneas was not there, he had been sent away as usual. I felt there was no point in telling anyone anything that was happening inside me. We had to win this war, and I, the king's daughter, believed in it less and less. I was in a fix. Whom could I talk to about that?

On top of this, the progress of the war seemed not to bear me out. Troy was holding its ground. This phrase was a bit too grand, because for some time it was not under threat. The Greeks were plundering the islands and the coastal cities some distance away. They left nothing behind their strong wooden fortifications but a couple of ships, tents, and a small guard troop – too strong for us to destroy them, too weak to attack us. What deprived me of hope was the very way we had gotten used to this state of affairs. How could a Trojan laugh when the enemy lurked outside his gates? And the sunshine. Always sunshine. Phoebus Apollo, darkly radiant, overpowering. The always identical places between which my life elapsed. The shrine. The temple grove, dry that year: the Scamander, which used to irrigate our garden, had dried up. My clay hut, my bed, chair, and table – the quarters I used at times when service to the temple forbade me to leave its precincts. The path to the fortress, sloping gently upward, always accompanied by two guards who were supposed to follow two steps behind me and did not speak with me because I did not permit it. The gate in the wall. The cry of the guards, always a different silly password to which the sentries above gave a silly reply. 'Down with the enemy!' 'Send them to blazes!' That kind of thing. Then the scrutiny of the officer of the watch. The sign for the gate to be opened. Always the same tedious route to the palace, always the same faces outside the craftsmen's houses. And when I had entered the palace, the always identical corridors leading to the always identical rooms. Only the people I met seemed to me more and more alien. To this day I do not know how I managed not to notice that I was a captive. That I was working under compulsion the way prisoners work. That my limbs no longer moved of their own free will, that I had lost all desire to walk, breathe, sing. Everything required a long-drawn-out act of decision. 'Get up!'

I ordered myself. 'Now walk!' And what an effort everything was. The unloved duty inside me ate up all my joy. Troy was impregnable to the enemy; it became so for me as well.

Figures move through this unmoving picture. Many have no names. That was the time when I forgot names quickly and had trouble learning new ones. All of a sudden there were many old people, old men. I used to run into them in the corridors of the palace, which at other times were totally deserted: half-crippled mummies, laboriously pushed along by slaves. They were going to the council. Then I also used to see my brothers, who otherwise spent their time with the troops: Hector-Dim-Cloud, who always spoke to me, wanted to hear how I was, how the women were; who entrusted Andromache, whom he loved deeply, to our protection. And Paris, crushed, smiling a crooked smile, only the shell of his former self, but more sharp-edged than ever. I was told he would stop at nothing – not where Greeks were concerned but Trojans; a dangerous man. He had one disgrace after another to make up for, all his life. He was not one you could count on. (Yes. It was then that I began – I could not seem to help myself – to divide the people I met into two groups in view of an unknown future emergency. You can count on him, but not on him. What was I doing it for? I did not want to know. Later it turned out that I had rarely been wrong.)

And King Priam, my father. He was a special case, and special to me. He crumbled. That was the word. King Priam crumbled as increasingly he was forced to flaunt his rank as king. He sat stiffly at the great celebrations in the hall court, in a seat which recently had been elevated beside and above Hecuba, and listened to the hymns in his praise. In his praise and in praise of the heroic deeds of the Trojans. New minstrels had sprung up; or the old ones, if they were still tolerated, changed their text. The new texts were glory-gabbing, showy, and sycophantic. Impossible that I was the only one who noticed that. I looked around me: the lustreless faces. They had themselves under tight rein. Did we have to behave this way? 'Yes,' said Panthous, with whom I had begun to talk again sometimes, because I had no one else. He told me the gist of the directive which had just been issued to the high priests of all the temples: the emphasis in all ceremonies was to be shifted from the dead heroes to the living ones. I was dismayed. Our faith, our self-confidence was founded on the veneration of dead heroes. It was they whom we invoked when we said 'eternal' and 'infinite.' Their greatness, which we regarded as unattainable, made us, the living, modest. That was just the point. 'Do you believe,' Panthous said, 'that modest heroes who can hope to achieve glory only after death are the right opponents for the immodest Greeks? Don't you think it more prudent to sing of the living heroes rather than the dead ones, and thus avoid revealing how many have already been killed?' 'But don't you see how much more dangerous it is to agitate the foundations of our unity carelessly!' I said. 'That you of all people should say that, Cassandra,' said Panthous. 'You yourself believe in nothing. Just like Eumelos and his men, who are at the bottom of everything. How are you any different from them?'

Coolly I set him straight. Would this Greek man reprimand a Trojan woman? How could I prove to him, or to myself, that he was wrong? At night I did not sleep. The headache began. What did I believe in, anyway?

If you can hear me, listen now, Aeneas. We never got this matter clear. I still have to explain it to you. No, I did not feel a twinge at your behaviour; I understood why you were withdrawn even when you were with me, even when you lay with me; I understood that you could no longer bear to listen to my foolish, never-ending protest: 'I want the same thing they do!' The only thing is, why did you not contradict me? Why did you not spare me forgetting myself so far as to say the same thing to Eumelos himself, when he and I had our first truly open, bitter confrontation?

It was after Achilles the brute had captured our poor brother Lycaon and sold him to the odious king of Lemnos in exchange for a precious bronze vessel – an insult that made Priam groan aloud. There seemed to be only one person in the citadel who knew how to answer the infamous presumption of the enemy: that man was Eumelos. He tightened the screws. He cast his security net (which hitherto had strangled the royal household and the civil service) across all of Troy; now it applied to everyone. The citadel was locked after darkness fell. Strict personal searches whenever Eumelos deemed necessary. Special authorisations for the security personnel.

'Eumelos,' I said, 'that is impossible.' (Naturally I knew that it was possible.) 'And why?' he asked with icy politeness. 'Because by doing that we'll be hurting ourselves more than the Greeks.' 'I'd like to hear you say that again,' he said. Fear gripped me then. 'Eumelos,' I cried imploringly – I am still ashamed of that – 'Please believe me! I want the same thing you people do.'

He pursed his lips tightly. I could not win him over. He said formally: 'Excellent. Then you will support our measures.' He left me standing there like a dumb clod. He was nearing the height of his power.

Why was I so downcast? So downcast that I got involved in an interior dialogue with Eumelos – with Eumelos! – that went on for days and nights? Things had come to a sorry pass. I wanted to convince Eumelos. But of what! That is what you asked me, Aeneas; I was mute. Today I would say I wanted to convince him that we could not become like Achilles, just to save ourselves. To convince him that it was not yet proved that, just to save ourselves, we had to become like the Greeks. And even if it were proved, wasn't it more important to live in our own way, by our own law, than just to live? But who was I trying to fool? For was it true, what I said? Wasn't it more important to survive? Wasn't that the most important thing of all? The only thing that mattered? Does that mean that Eumelos was the man of the hour?

But what if for a long time we had been facing a different question altogether: whether to take on the enemy's face knowing that we would be destroyed anyhow?

Listen, Aeneas. Please understand me. I could not go through that again. Many days I lay on my bed, drank a little goat's milk, had the windows draped, closed my eyes, and remained motionless, simply not to remind the animal who was tearing at my brain of my existence. Marpessa walked very softly up and down; she fetched Oenone, who gently stroked my forehead and neck as only she knew how. Her hands were always cold now. Was winter coming already?

Yes, winter was coming. The great autumn market had been held outside the gates, the ghost of a market. The vendors were Eumelos's men in disguise; the real vendors stood among them, frozen. The customers were Eumelos's men in disguise; we, the customers, stood among them fumbling with terror. Who was acting whose part? In tight formations, insecure, impudent, the Greeks. By chance I was wedged in next to Agamemnon while he bought a very expensive, beautiful necklace from a goldsmith without haggling over the price. And then he bought a second, identical necklace and held it out to me: 'Isn't it beautiful?' A deathly silence stretching from horizon to horizon surrounded us. I said quietly, almost amiably: 'Yes. It's very beautiful, Agamemnon.' 'You know me,' said Agamemnon. 'How should I not?' He looked at me strangely for a long time; I could not interpret his gaze. Then he said softly, so that only I could understand him: 'For the life of me I'd like to give this to my daughter. She is no more. Somehow she resembled you. You take it.' Then he gave me the necklace and left hurriedly.

None of my family ever mentioned this necklace. I wore it sometimes, I am wearing it still. A little while ago I saw its mate around Clytemnestra's neck; she saw the mate of hers around mine. We reached up to touch our necklaces with an identical gesture, looked at each other, agreed as only women agree.

I asked Panthous in passing: 'Which daughter was that?' 'Iphigenia,' he said. 'And it's true what they say about her?' 'Yes. He sacrificed her. Your Calchas ordered him to.'

They act in haste and foolishly. Believe the incredible. Do what they do not want to do, and mourn their victims with self-pity.

The fear is back again.

New troops from outlying provinces had arrived in the citadel, you often saw black and brown faces in the streets now, troops of warriors squatted everywhere around campfires; all of a sudden it was no longer advisable for us women to be out alone. If you saw it properly – only no one ventured to do that – the men of both sides seemed to have joined forces against our women. Demoralised, they withdrew into the winter caves of their houses, to the glowing fires and the children. In the temple they prayed with a fervour that displeased me because they wanted our god Apollo to serve as substitute for their stolen life. I could not stand it any longer. Protected by my priestess's robes, I went to see Anchises again. Whenever I came to see him after a long interval away, I felt as if my visits to him had never been interrupted. Admittedly, two young women whom I did not know got up and left, in a natural way, without embarrassment; but it hurt nonetheless. Anchises had just begun to weave those tall baskets. Everyone took it as a whim, but now that you are on the road, Aeneas, where could you have stowed your supplies, where could you have carried your father, light as he has become now, if not in a basket of this kind?

So he did not stop preparing the reeds while we talked. We always began by talking about remote subjects. He always served me that wine from Mount Ida that got into my blood, and flat barley cakes he had baked himself. I told him word for word the conversation I had had with Eumelos.

Then he jumped up, threw his bald head back, and

roared with laughter. 'Yes! I can well believe it! That's just like the scalawag!'

Whenever he laughed I used to laugh with him. Already everything was easier, but the most important part was still to come; Anchises instructed me. When he instructed me he used to call me 'girl.' 'So, girl, pay attention now. Eumelos needs Achilles the way one old shoe needs the other. But there is a primitive trick behind it, a flaw in his reasoning which he has passed on to you in all his diabolical innocence. And this trick can work only so long as you do not come on its weak point. Namely: he is presupposing what he had still to create: war. Once he has gotten that far, he can take this war as the normal state and presuppose that there is only one way out: victory. In this case, of course, the enemy dictates the courses open to you. Then you are caught in a vice and you have to choose between two evils, Achilles and Eumelos. Don't you see, girl, how Achilles has come along at just the right time for Eumelos? How he could not wish for a better adversary than that fiend?'

Yes, yes, I saw. I was grateful to Anchises, drew the conclusions he left me to draw. So we ought to have arrested the evil before its name became 'war.' We ought not to have let Eumelos become established. We – who then? The king, Priam, my father. The conflict for me remained. It had been shifted from Eumelos to King Priam. And in the conflict lay the fear.

I was afraid, Aeneas. That was the thing you were never willing to believe. You did not know what that kind of fear was. I have a fear-memory. A feeling-memory. How often you laughed, when you returned from one of your many journeys, because I could not give you the kind of report of events you expected. Who had killed whom by what methods, who was rising or falling in the hierarchy, who had fallen in love with whom, who had stolen whose wife: you had to ask other people to find out these things. I knew it all of course, that was not the point. It is those who are not involved in events who learn most about them. But although I did not wish it, my memory simply did not take these facts seriously enough. As if they were not real. Not real enough. As if they were shadow-deeds. How can I explain to you? I will give you an example. Polyxena.

Oh, Aeneas. I can see her every feature as if she were standing before me, her face in which misfortune was inscribed: how was it that I could see that? And how was it that I could hear that undertone to her voice which inspired my melting fear that my sister would come to a bad end? How often I felt like grabbing her hands and shrieking aloud what I saw. Why did I hold back? Why did I brace all my muscles against this fear-based certainty? No one need tell me why the birth of the twins was so difficult. My muscles have turned hard. I had the feeling that I was screening with my body the place through which, unbeknown to everyone but me, other realities were seeping into our solid-bodied world, realities which our five agreed-upon senses do not grasp: for which reason we must deny them.

Words. Everything I tried to convey about that experience was, and is, paraphrase. We have no name for what spoke out of me. I was its mouth, and not of my own free will. It had to subdue me before I would breathe a word it suggested. It was the enemy who spread the tale that I spoke 'the truth' and that you all would not listen to me. They did not spread it out of malice, that was just how they understood it. For the Greeks there is no alternative but either truth or lies, right or wrong, victory or defeat, friend or enemy, life or death. They think differently than we do. What cannot be seen, smelled, heard, touched, does not exist. It is the other alternative that they crush between their clear-cut distinctions, the third alternative, which in their view does not exist, the smiling vital force that is able to generate itself from itself over and over: the undivided, spirit in life, life in spirit. Anchises once said that the gift of empathy could be more important for the Greeks than the accursed invention of iron. If only they could embrace someone besides themselves within the iron concepts of good and evil. Us, for example.

Their singers will pass on none of all this.

And what if they – or we – did pass it on? What would be the result? Nothing. Unfortunately or fortunately, nothing. Not song, only commands do more than stir the air. That is not my tenet, it is Penthesilea's. She despised what she called my 'affectations.' 'Your dreams against their javelins!' she said. She had an awkward, miserable way of laughing. I would have been only too happy to prove my point to her. She turned out to be right, you might say, if there is any right on the side of the javelins. I understood too late (once again too late!) that she offered herself, her life, her body, to carry the wrong too far in the sight of us all. The abyss of hopelessness in which she lived.

One day Hecuba and Polyxena came into the temple just at the time I was serving there. The strange thing was that they wanted to sacrifice to Apollo and not, as they usually preferred, to our protectress Athena, whose temple was much more conveniently located in the city. They did not tell me the purpose of their sacrifice – fruits of the field. I saw only how at one they were, and my heart contracted. Their appeal to the deity – I learned much, much later – was so unnatural that they could not make it to a goddess but only to a male god: Polyxena feared she was pregnant, and they asked Apollo to take the pregnancy from her. She wanted no child by Andron, to whom she was as much a slave as ever. Why did the conflict she lived with appear on her face in that hour as a fragile, beseeching expression? Why did Achilles the brute have to see that expression? My breath stopped cold when he walked in. He had kept away from Apollo ever since he had killed my brother Troilus here, even though – regrettably in my opinion – negotiations had determined that this temple was to be a neutral place, open to the Greeks too, for the purposes of worshipping their god. So in he came, Achilles the brute, and saw my sister Polyxena; and I, from the altar where you can see everything, saw that he saw her. How much she resembled our brother Troilus. How Achilles devoured her with his hideous glances, which I knew well. I think I whispered: 'Polyxena.' Then dropped in a faint. When I woke up, leather-cheeked old Herophile sat beside me. 'She is lost, Polyxena is lost,' I said. 'Get up, Cassandra,' said Herophile. 'Pull yourself together. Don't let yourself go like that. Now is not the time for visions. What is supposed to happen, happens. We are not here to prevent it. So don't make a fuss.'

All of a sudden our temple became a much-sought-after spot. Lower-level negotiators met there, to arrange the crucial rendezvous: the Trojan Hector met the Greek hero Achilles. I stayed in the chamber behind the altar, where you can hear every word. I heard what I already knew: the Greek hero Achilles wanted the Trojan princess Polyxena. Hector, who had learned from Panthous that among the Greeks fathers and elder brothers exercise authority over their daughters and sisters, seemed to go along with Achilles' wishes, as it was agreed he should. Fine, he said, he would hand over his sister if Achilles in turn would reveal to us the layout of the Greek camp. I thought I had heard him wrong. Never before had Troy demanded of an adversary that he betray his own people. Never had it sold one of its daughters to the enemy at such a price. Andron, to whom Polyxena was so attached, stood motionless behind brother Hector. And Achilles the brute, though he had proved that he did not fear the sanctuary, did not go for either of their throats. Could he suspect how closely the first ring of armed men had surrounded the shrine? Hardly. He said he would consider the whole thing; but he would like to be allowed to see Polyxena once more. Strange to say, brother Hector did not want to permit this. Then friend Andron intervened with his sprightly voice. 'Why ever not!' I heard him say. Oh, Sister, I thought, if only you could hear him, your pretty good-for-nothing. It was agreed that that evening Polyxena would show herself to her future owner on the wall beside the Scaean Gate.

I begged Polyxena not to show herself. 'Why ever not?' she said, just like Andron. So she had no reason not to; but was that enough? What positive reason did she have? 'Do you love this brute? Are you capable even of that!' I said before I could stop myself. That is the sentence I cannot forgive myself for. It transported my sister beyond my reach. I saw it at once, by the expression on her face: transported. In panic I grabbed her hands, apologised, kept on at her as if I were out of my senses. In vain. In the evening before sunset she stood on the wall wearing that new, remote smile, and looked down on Achilles. He stared. He was almost drooling. Then my sister Polyxena slowly bared her breast, while at the same time – still with that faraway gaze – she looked at us: her lover, her brother, her sister. I answered her look imploringly. 'Hey, Hector!' Achilles the brute roared up at us in a hoarse voice. 'Do you hear me? I agree to your terms.'

The terms were agreed upon. For months my sister Polyxena was the most admired woman in Troy. She had wanted that – to punish those she loved by ruining herself. The deeds the war gave birth to were abortions. When she offered her breast to the Greek, Polyxena had lost Andron's child in the form of a little clot of blood. Triumphantly, shamelessly, she made it known. She was free, she said, free. Nothing, no one had a hold on her.

That is how it was.

I went to Anchises. The company I used to meet with were still there. My suspicion was correct: slave women from the Greek camp used to meet here with the women from our city. And why not? It took more than that to surprise me nowadays. So I thought. Then they surprised me, after all. We learned that Achilles had absolutely refused to go on fighting for the Greeks. Plague had overrun the Greek camp; the seer Calchas claimed it had been sent by the god Apollo. A little slave girl whom the great Agamemnon regarded as his property must (Calchas said) be restored to her father, who also happened to be a seer. Agamemnon had to be indemnified for his loss. No doubt with some assistance from her father Calchas, Briseis, our Briseis, was taken away from Achilles, who for so long had been free to do as he liked with her, and assigned to the great fleet commander, Agamemnon. The slave girls said he kept her in a special tent. That he did not visit her either by day or by night. The only man who visited her, they said, was her father Calchas, who had gone completely grey. When I ventured to ask how she was, the only reply was a long mute look.

I was freezing. I felt cold to the innermost fibre of my body. Anchises seemed to know how I felt. 'Aeneas is coming,' he said softly. 'Did you already know?' Then warm blood pumped into my face. Aeneas came. His ship got through. I was alive. Aeneas was depressed. He had been drawn into the war completely. He had brought hope of reinforcements. Delaying tactics had to be employed against the Greeks. Single combats were held between some of their men and some of ours. Actually they were athletic contests fought by rules acceptable to the Greeks. All Troy stood along the wall watching the duel between our Hector and Ajax the Great – a particular pleasure because we saw that Hector's tenacious training had paid off. As a fighter Hector-Dim-Cloud was a match for anyone. Hecuba went away, white-faced. The two heroes exchanged their arms, and the fools along the walls applauded. Arms of woe. Achilles the brute used Ajax's sword-belt to tie Hector to his chariot when he dragged him around the citadel. And Ajax the Great used Hector's sword to commit suicide when he was preyed on by madness.

Objects slipped out of our hands and turned against us, so then we attributed exaggerated significance to them. What expense went into the manufacture of Hector's shield, sword, javelin, and armour! He was entitled (it was said) not only to the best weapons but also to the most beautiful. Once I ran into him – early spring was already in the air – outside the armourers' door. He joined me notwithstanding our accompaniment by Eumelos's guards. Sometimes a single conversation is enough. It turned out that he had been observing me. 'You seem to be drifting away from me, Sister,' he said, without reproach in his voice. 'But do you know where you're going?' No question had touched me so much for a long time. Hector. Dear one. He knew that he only had a short time to live. I knew that he knew. What could I have said to him? I told him that Troy was no longer Troy. That I did not know how to deal with that. That I felt like an injured animal in a trap, seeing no way out. Whenever I think of Hector I feel the edge of the wall down my back as I pressed up against it, and smell horse dung mixed with earth. He put his arm around my shoulder, drew me to him. 'Little sister. Always so exacting. Always such grand aims. Maybe you have to be that way, we have to put up with you. Too bad you're not a man. You could go and fight. Believe me, sometimes that's better.' Better than what? We smiled.

Otherwise only our eyes spoke. Said that we loved each other. That we had to say goodbye to each other. Never again, Hector, dear one, did I want to be a man. I often thanked those powers which answer for our sex that I was allowed to be a woman. That I did not have to be present on the day we both knew you would fall; that I could avoid the battlefield where Achilles was up to his old mischief after our men killed his dearest friend, Patroclus. Achilles' slave girl came to Anchises, her features distorted. In order to appease her obstinate master, Agamemnon had brought Briseis, our Briseis, back to him personally. In what a state! The girl was weeping. No, she would never go back. Let us do what we liked with her. Arisbe made a sign to the charming Oenone. This young slave girl, who asked us to hide her, marked the beginning of the free and easy life in the caves. Next summer I saw her again; she was a changed person. I, too, was ready to become that changed person who had been stirring inside me for so long already, underneath the despair, pain, and grief. The first stirring I allowed was the stab of envy when the slave girl of Achilles went off I knew not where, clasping Oenone tightly. 'What about me? Save me too!' I almost cried. But I had still to experience what lay in store for me: the day when I lay on my wickerwork bed in a cold sweat knowing that Hector was entering the battlefield, and knowing that he was being killed.

I do not know how it happened; no one was ever allowed to tell me about it, not even Aeneas, who was present, although I felt no concern for his safety. In the deepest depths, in the innermost core of me, where body and soul are not yet divided and where not a single word or a single thought can penetrate, I experienced the whole of Hector's fight, his wounding, his tenacious resistance, and his death. It is not too much to say that I *was* Hector: because it would not be nearly enough to say I was joined with him. Achilles the brute stabbed him to death, stabbed me to death; mutilated him, fastened him on to his chariot by Ajax's sword-belt, dragged him many times around the fortress. I was, living, what Hector became dead: a chunk of raw meat. Insensible. My mother's shrieks, my father's howls: far away. Should he entreat Achilles to give him back the corpse, the king wanted to know. Why ever not? The way my father walked the floor at night. If I had still been I, it would have moved me infinitely. It moved me a little that when he came across Achilles sleeping, he could not bring himself to assault him treacherously. Then I was standing unmoved on the wall once more, at the familiar spot beside the Scaean Gate. Below were the scales. On one side of the scales was a mass of raw meat that had once been our brother Hector; and on the other all the gold we had, for Hector's murderer. This was the low point or the high point of the war. The coldness inside me. Andromache lying inanimate on the ground. And Polyxena's face, which suited this occasion, the voluptuousness of self-destruction. The contemptuous way she threw her bracelets and chains onto the mountain of gold, which still fell a little short of the weight of Hector's corpse. We were learning new things at a dazzling rate. Until now we did not know that dead people were worth their weight in gold. Then we learned another new thing: you could exchange a living woman for a dead man. Achilles shouted up to Priam: 'Hey, King! Give me your beautiful daughter Polyxena and keep your gold.'

Polyxena's laughter. And the king's reply, quickly agreed upon with Eumelos and Andron: 'Persuade Menelaus to give up Helen, and you can have my daughter Polyxena.'

From that day on I stopped dreaming, a bad sign. That day and the following night, that part of me from which dreams come, even bad dreams, was destroyed. Achilles the brute occupied every inch of space outside and inside us. That night, when he cremated the body of his darling Patroclus, Achilles the brute butchered twelve captives as a sacrifice, the noblest born, among them two sons of Hecuba and Priam. That night the gods abandoned us. Twelve times the cry, that of an animal. Each time my mother's fingernails dug deeper into my flesh. Then thirteen funeral pyres – one enormous and twelve smaller ones – sent their crackling, dreadful red flames against the black sky. There was a smell of charred flesh; the wind was coming from the sea. Twelve times the red-hot iron burned out of us that place from which pain, love, life, dreams can come. The nameless softness that makes human beings human. When Hecuba dropped behind me, she was an old woman, hollow-cheeked, white-haired. Andromache a whimpering bundle in the corner. Polyxena sharp and resolute like a sword. Priam, devoid of all royalty, a sick old man.

Troy lay dark, deathly still. A troop of our warriors, led by my brother Paris, stormed into the cellar rooms of the citadel where the Greek captives crouched shaking with fear. One of the palace maidservants came and fetched me. I went into the cellar, which stank of decay, sweat, and excrement. The Trojans and the Greek captives stood facing each other in trembling silence, separated by an abyss one step wide; above the abyss the bright blades of the Trojans. Then I walked, without my priestly garments, along the narrow interval, grazed by the hot breath of the Greeks, the cold blades of the Trojans; step by step, from one wall to the other. Everything still. Behind me the Trojan blades lowered. The Greeks wept. How I loved my countrymen.

Paris blocked my way at the exit. So, Priestess, you

do not permit my men to repay deeds in kind. I said: No.

That was almost the only word left for me to say.

Panthous drew my attention to the fact that words have physical effects. 'No' had a contracting, 'yes' a relaxing, effect. However did it happen, why did I let it happen, why did Aeneas stay away so long? Panthous approached me again. Even though we could no longer stand each other. I got angry for no reason when I merely looked at him – narrow, shrunken, wearing the women's garments of the priest, and the big head on top. Always the cynical grin. I did not like people on whom you could smell the fear. He could not bear compassion that had contempt in it. Without my noticing, spring had come again. We were standing under the olive trees in the grove of Apollo, at evening. It had struck me that I never saw Panthous any more except in the vicinity of the temple. 'Yes,' he said. 'Beyond this fence begins the wilderness. The danger.' I took a long, thorough look at him. Which animal did he resemble now? A threatened polecat. Drawing his lips back from his teeth in fear, in seeming disgust, and baring his eyeteeth. Attacking because he is afraid. I felt sick. An image came over me, I could not stave it off. People with clubs were driving a polecat out of his den, through the temple precincts, chasing him out of the reserve and killing him; he died with a whistling, hissing sound. He saw the dismay in my eyes and threw himself on me, buried me underneath him, stammered my name into my ear, begged for help. I gave in to him. Responded to him. He failed. In his rage and disappointment he hissed like the animal.

It came out that I had saved his life that night along with the others: he had been in the cellar among the captive Greeks. He could not forgive me for not having been afraid of the sword blades. 'You people won't get me,' he hissed. 'The Greeks won't get me, either.' He showed me the capsule with the powder. He was right. We did not get him, nor did the Greeks – the Amazons got him.

Penthesilea's women. Aeneas (it now appeared) had led them here by a safe route. He, with his white hands, walked along beside dark Penthesilea with her wild black hair that stood out from her head in all directions. Was I deceived, or did Aeneas's gaze cling to her? Then came Myrine, little pony, out of breath at the end of a long race that had no further destination. What did that woman want in Troy? People told me, Aeneas told me: 'She is looking for battle.' So had we reached the point that anyone who was looking for a battle, man or woman, was welcome here? Aeneas said, 'Yes, we have reached that point.' He expressed very guarded views of the small, tightly knit band of women. Guardedly we lay side by side, talking about Penthesilea. It was crazy. I could not say a word about the night when the

Greeks killed the captives. Aeneas did not ask. His body glowed white, white in the darkness. He touched me. Nothing stirred. I wept. Aeneas wept. They had finished us. Desolately we parted. Dear one. When we really parted later on, there were no tears, no comfort either. Something like anger on your side, resolution on mine; each of us understood the other. We were not yet through with each other. To separate that way is harder, easier.

These words have no meaning for us. Harder, easier. How can you draw such fine distinctions when everything has become unbearable?

What does that mean? What is going on? What do these people want? My chariot driver is leading old women and men to me (apparently secretly), old people from Mycenae who seem to approach me with reverence. 'Marpessa, do you see that?' 'I see it, Cassandra.' 'Can you guess what they want?' 'As well as you do.' 'I don't want to.' 'Tell them, but it won't help.' Our chariot driver is acting as their spokesman. They want me to tell them the fate of their city.

Poor people.

How they resemble my Trojans.

Do you see, Aeneas, that is what I meant: the same thing all over again.

If I tell them I know nothing, they will not believe me. If I tell them what I see coming, which anyone else could do as well, they will kill me. That would not be such a bad thing, but their own queen would punish them for it. Or does no one have me under surveillance here as they did in Troy? What if in captivity I am free to express myself? Dear enemies. Who am I to see you as nothing but the victors, instead of as the ones who will live? The ones who must live so that what we call life will continue. These poor victors must live on for all the people they have killed.

I tell them: 'If you can stop being victorious, this your city will endure.'

'Permit me a question, Seeress,' (the chariot driver). 'Ask.' 'You do not believe that, do you?' 'Believe what?' 'That we can stop being victorious.' 'I do not know of any victor who could stop.' 'So if victory after victory means destruction in the end, then destruction is planted in our nature?'

The question of questions. What a shrewd man.

'Come closer, Chariot Driver. Listen. I believe that we do not know our nature. That I do not know anything. So in the future there may be people who know how to turn their victory into life.'

'In the future, Seeress. I am asking about Mycenae. About myself and my children. About our royal house.'

I am silent. I see the corpse of his king, drained of blood like a head of livestock at the butcher's. I tremble. The chariot driver, suddenly pale, steps back. I must say nothing more to him.

It will not be long now.

Who was Penthesilea? Clearly I did not give her enough credit, and she did not give enough credit to me. Sharp-eyed and sharp-tongued, she was a shade too strident for my taste. Her every appearance, her every sentence, was a challenge to someone. She was not looking for allies among us. She was not merely fighting the Greeks; she was fighting all men. I saw that Priam was afraid of her, and Eumelos surrounded her with a thick security cordon. But the dread the common people felt at her unqualified attitudes surrounded her more impenetrably than any screening service. We suspected, but mostly did not want to know, what things lay behind her that still lay ahead of us. 'Better to die fighting than to be made slaves,' her women said. She had them all in the palm of her hand and would incite or pacify them however she chose, by moving her little finger. She ruled as only kings rule. The worthy Trojans whispered in horror that these women had killed their own menfolk. They were monsters with only one breast (it was said), who had burned out the other at a tender age in order to use their bows more efficiently. Thereupon they appeared bare-trunked in the temple of Athena, showing their beautiful naked breasts and carrying their weapons. 'Artemis,' they said – that is what they called Pallas Athena – 'carries a spear herself; she would not want us to come to her unarmed.' The priests sent all the Trojans out of the temple and let the warrior women have it for their wild rituals. 'They kill whomever they love, love in order to kill,' said Panthous. Strange to say, I ran into Penthesilea and Myrine at Anchises's place. Normally they could not stand to have men anywhere near them. They put up with Anchises, who looked at them with a wily and unprejudiced gaze. All the women I knew were there. They said they wanted to get to know each other.

It turned out that in many ways they were at one. I say 'they,' for I held back at first. That part of the inhabited world which we knew had turned against us ever more cruelly, ever more swiftly. 'Against us women,' said Penthesilea. 'Against us people,' Arisbe replied.

PENTHESILEA: The men are getting what they paid for.

ARISBE: You call it getting what they paid for when they are reduced to the level of butchers?

PENTHESILEA: They are butchers. So they are doing what they enjoy.

ARISBE: And what about us? What if we became butchers, too?

PENTHESILEA: Then we are doing what we have to do. But we don't enjoy it.

ARISBE: We should do what they do in order to show that we are different?

PENTHESILEA: Yes.

OENONE: But one can't live that way.

PENTHESILEA: Not live? You can die all right.

HECUBA: Child, you want everything to come to a stop.

PENTHESILEA: That is what I want. Because I don't know any other way to make the men stop.

Then the young slave woman from the Greek camp came over to her, knelt down before her, and laid Penthesilea's hands against her face. She said: 'Penthesilea. Come join us.' 'Join you? What does that mean?' 'Come to the mountains. The forest. The caves along the Scamander. Between killing and dying there is a third alternative: living.'

The young slave woman's remark cut me to the quick. So they were living. Without me. They knew each other. The girl I called the 'young slave woman' was called Killa. It seemed that Oenone (whom I never saw in Paris's vicinity any more) was her friend, they suited each other. Marpessa, my servant, seemed to enjoy great respect in that world. Oh, to be part of it! The same bright longing in Myrine's eyes. It was the first open look we afforded each other.

PENTHESILEA: 'No.' The spark in Myrine's eyes went out at once. Violently I reproached Penthesilea: 'You want to die, and you are forcing the others to accompany you.'

That is the second sentence I regret.

'What!' shrieked Penthesilea. 'You speak to me like that! You of all people: neither fish nor fowl!'

It would not have taken much for us to fly at each other's throat.

I had forgotten all that until now. Because I did not want to admit that a woman could crave death. And because her death made ash of everything we had known of her before. We had believed that the terror could not increase, but now we had to recognise that there are no limits to the atrocities people can inflict on one another; that we are capable of rummaging through someone else's entrails and of cracking his skull, trying to find out what causes the most pain. I say 'we,' and of all the 'we's' I eventually said, this is still the one that challenges me most. It is so much easier to say 'Achilles the brute' than to say this 'we.'

Why am I moaning? Marpessa was there – you were there, Marpessa, when Myrine, a bloody heap, scratched at the door of the hut where we had taken refuge. It was black as death, no fires burned that night to light it up, the dead were not gathered until morning. There was not a single spot on Myrine's body where we could touch her without her moaning with pain. I can still see the face of the farm woman in whose hut we found shelter, while Myrine lay before us and we dabbed her wounds with an herbal juice. We – you and I, Marpessa – had no tears. I was hoping it would be over quickly. When we heard the Greeks entering these huts for the first time in their search for Amazon stragglers, we threw a mountain of unspun wool over Myrine in the corner: her little scrap of breath did not stir the mountain. We squatted around the fire in filthy, torn clothing. I remember that I was sharpening a knife to cut up vegetables, and that when a Greek burst in, his gaze fell on the knife at the same moment mine did. Then we looked at each other. He had understood me. He did not touch me. To save face he took away with him the goat that Anchises had carved, which had stood in a wall niche. Weeks later, when Myrine became aware of what had happened, she could not forgive herself for having been saved. She would not say a word but Penthesilea's name. Yes, I am moaning again the way we moaned then whenever we thought or heard that name. Myrine did not leave her side during the battle. When Achilles was taking Penthesilea to task, five men held Myrine; I saw the haemorrhages under her skin. Other women told us about it, not Myrine. Achilles was beside himself with amazement when he ran across Penthesilea during the battle. He began to play with her, she thrust at him. They say that Achilles shook himself; he must have believed he was out of his mind. A woman – greeting him with a sword! The fact that she forced him to take her seriously was her last triumph. They fought for a long time; all the Amazons had been thrust away from Penthesilea. He threw her down, wanted to take her captive; she scratched him with her dagger and forced him to kill her. The gods be praised for that if for nothing else.

I can see what happened next as if I had been present. Achilles the Greek hero desecrates the dead woman. The man, incapable of loving the living woman, hurls himself on the dead victim so that he can go on killing her. And I moan. Why? She did not feel it. We felt it, all of us women. What will become of us if that spreads? The men, weak, whipped up into victors, need us as victims in order not to stop feeling altogether. Where is that leading? Even the Greeks felt that Achilles had gone too far. So they went further in order to punish him: had horses drag the dead woman across the field – he wept for her now – and throw her into the river. Flay the woman in order to strike at the man.

Yes. Yes. Yes. A monster was on the loose and raged through the camps. White-eyed, its features distorted, it raged in the van of the formation that carried Penthesilea's corpse, and kept growing larger on the way from the river where they had pulled her out. Amazons, Trojan women, nothing but women. A procession leading nowhere on earth: leading to madness. Not one Greek was to be seen. When they reached the temple, where I was doing the service, they were no longer recognisable. The companions of the corpse came to resemble human beings as little as she did. Not to speak of the howling. They were at the end of their tether and they knew it; but knowledge had wiped out the zone in which one knows. Their knowledge was in their flesh, which hurt unbearably – the howling! – in their hair, teeth, fingernails, in the marrow of their bones. They suffered beyond all measure, and suffering like that has its own law. 'Everything it gives rise to falls on the heads of those who caused it': that is what I said later to the council. At the time, facing the women, facing the corpse, I was torn by an anguish that never left me afterward, no matter what happened. I learned to laugh again – unbelievable miracle – but the anguish remained. This is the end of us.

They laid Penthesilea under a willow tree. They wanted me to begin the dirge. I did so, softly, in a broken voice. The women, standing in a circle, chimed in shrilly. Began to sway. Sang louder, twitched. One threw back her head, the others followed. Their bodies convulsed. One woman staggered inside the circle, began to dance beside the corpse, stamping her feet, throwing out her arms and shaking. The screeches grew deafening. The woman inside the circle lost control of herself. Her mouth was wide open and foaming. Two, three, four other women lost control of their limbs, reached the point where the pinnacle of pain is indistinguishable from the pinnacle of pleasure. I felt the rhythm transfer itself to me. As the dance began inside me, I felt a strong temptation to abandon myself now, when things were beyond help, and exit from time. The rhythm told me that my feet preferred to exit from time, and I was about to surrender to it completely. Let the wilderness engulf us again. Let the undivided, the unmanifested, the primal cause, devour us. Dance, Cassandra, move! Yes, I am coming. Everything in me urged its way toward them.

But then the wretched Panthous appeared. 'Go

away!' I screamed, and at the same time a Trojan woman screamed: 'A Greek!' The rhythm broke down. Keen, dead sober, plans to save him sped through me. Divert the women, hide the man. Too late. Eumelos! Not there. Why not. The gift of prophecy! Apollo, do not let down your priestess now, let her save your priest. I raised my arms, closed my eyes, shrieked as loudly as I could: 'Apollo! Apollo!'

Panthous had already turned to run away. If only he had stood still! Maybe the women would have followed me, not him. For several seconds there was a deathly stillness. Then this shriek, a shriek of murder and despair. They ran me down. I lay there for dead beside dead Penthesilea. Sister, I envy you the fact that you cannot hear. I heard. The drumming steps of the pursuers. The moment they stopped. The hiss, the hiss of the polecat. The sound of wood striking flesh. The cracking of a skull. And then the stillness. 'Penthesilea, let's exchange places. Hey, my dear. Nothing is sweeter than death. Come, my friend, and give me your aid. I cannot go on.'

I was very light to carry, Aeneas said later. No, he did not mind having to carry me so far. What hurt him was the way I called him 'friend' with someone quite different in mind. He swore not to leave me alone any more. He kept the vow when he could. In the end I released him from it.

So I came to the women in the caves, carried in Aeneas's arms. 'Someone had to carry you to get you here,' they used to tease me later. 'Otherwise you would not come.'

Would I have stayed away otherwise? Out of arrogance? I do not know. It seemed, did it not, that everything was repeating itself, everything from that long-ago time when I was mad? My bed. The dark walls. Instead of the window a bright glow coming from the entrance. Arisbe present from time to time. Oenone almost continually. No one else in the world has hands like hers. No, I was not mad. Solace was what I needed. Peace that was not the peace of the grave. Living peace. Love's peace.

They did not stop me from disappearing inside myself completely. I did not speak. Hardly ate. Barely moved. Did not sleep, to begin with. Gave myself up to the pictures that had eaten their way into my head. 'Time must pass,' I heard Arisbe say. How could time help me? The pictures grew paler. For hours on end, I believe, Oenone's light hand stroked my forehead. At the same time I heard her murmurs, which I did not understand, did not need to understand. I fell asleep. Aeneas was sitting beside me, a fire was burning, the soup Marpessa brought me was fit for the gods. No one tried to spare me. No one behaved with constraint on my account. Anchises, who seemed to be living here too, spoke as loudly as ever and made the cave boom with his laughter. Only his body grew fragile, not his spirit. He needed adversaries, sought out Arisbe, began to fight with her but meant me. Arisbe, with her trumpeting voice, her stiff horse's hair, her red-veined face, gave him a piece of her mind. The fire flickered up the walls; what kind of stones were those? 'What kind of stones are those?' I said, astonished at how natural my voice sounded. Then there was a silence into which my voice fitted; now it had found exactly the space intended for it.

What kind of stones were those? Had I never seen them before today, then? They asked. They threw dry logs onto the fire to give me light. 'Figures? Yes.' Carved out of the stone longer ago than anyone could remember. Women, if I was not mistaken. Yes. A goddess in the centre; others making offerings to her. I recognised her now. Flowers lay before the stone, wine, ears of barley. Killa said reverently: 'Cybele.' I saw Arisbe smile.

That evening she sat with me while the others slept. We talked unreservedly, amiably, and matter-of-factly. 'Killa,' said Arisbe, 'needs to attach a name to the stone. Most women need to,' she said. 'Artemis, Cybele, Athena, some other name.' Well, they should do as they liked. Perhaps gradually, without even noticing it, they might come to take the names as a likeness. 'You mean the stones stand for something else.' 'Of course. Do you pray to the wooden Apollo?' 'I haven't for a long time now. But what do the images stand for?' 'That's the question. They stand for the things in us that we do not dare to recognise, that is how it seems to me. There are very few people with whom I discuss my thoughts about that. Why hurt other people? Or disturb them? If we had time . . . '

All of a sudden I noticed that my heart was in great pain. Tomorrow I would get up again with a re-animated heart that was no longer beyond the reach of pain.

'You think that man cannot see himself, Arisbe?' 'That's right. He cannot stand it. He needs the alien image.' 'And will that never change? Will the same thing always come again? Self-estrangement, idols, hatred?' 'I don't know. This much I do know: there are gaps in time. This is one of them, here and now. We cannot let it pass without taking advantage of it.'

There at last I had my 'we.'

I dreamed that night, after so many desolate nights without dreams. I saw colours, red and black, life and death. They interpenetrated, they did not fight each other as I would have expected even in a dream. They changed form continually, they continually produced new patterns, which could be unbelievably beautiful. They were like waters, like a sea. In the middle of the sea I saw a bright island which I was approaching rapidly in my dream – for I was flying; yes, I was flying! What was there on the island? What kind of creature? A human being? An animal? It glowed the way only Aeneas glows at night. What joy. Then headlong fall, breeze, darkness, awakening. Hecuba, my mother.

'Mother,' I said. 'I'm dreaming again.' 'Get up. Come with me. You are needed. They won't listen to me.'

So I was not to be allowed to stay? To stay here, where I felt at ease? Did that mean I was all well? Killa clung to me, begged: 'Come on, stay!' I looked at Arisbe, Anchises. Yes, I had to go.

Hecuba led me straight to the council. No. Wrong. To the hall where the council used to be held. Where conspirators crouched together now, led by King Priam. They refused to let us in. Hecuba declared that they – the king above all – would be responsible for the consequences if we were not admitted now. The messenger came back. We were to come in. But only for a short while. They had no time. For as long as I can remember the council had no time for matters of importance.

At first I could not hear because I was seeing my father. A ruin of a man. Did he know who I was? Was he drowsing?

The matter concerned Polyxena. No, it concerned Troy. No, it concerned Achilles the brute. It concerned the plan that Polyxena was supposed to lure Achilles into our temple. Into the temple of the Thymbraian Apollo. Under the pretext of wanting to marry him. One suspicion after another raced through my head. 'Marry? But— ' 'Nothing to worry about,' I was told. Just pretend. In reality—

I could not believe my ears. In reality our brother Paris would sally forth ('sally forth'! Paris himself used that term!) from behind the image of the god, where he would be hidden, and he would strike Achilles in his vulnerable spot: the heel. Why there specifically? He had confided his vulnerable spot to our sister Polyxena. And Polyxena? Was playing along. Naturally. 'How does she feel about it?' Paris asked insolently. 'She's looking forward to it.'

'That means you're using Polyxena as a decoy for Achilles.'

Broad grin. 'You've got it. That's it. Achilles will come into the temple without shoes: she insisted he fulfil that condition.'

Laughter all around.

'Alone?'

'Well, what do you think? Of course alone. And he will not leave the temple alive.'

'And Polyxena? Will she wait for him there alone?'

'Except for Paris,' said Eumelos. 'And except for us, of course. But we'll stand outside.'

'And so Achilles will embrace Polyxena there?'

'Make-believe. When his attention is sufficiently distracted' – laughter – 'Paris's arrow will strike him.'

Laughter.

'And Polyxena has agreed to this?'

'Agreed? She's eager for it. A real Trojan woman.'

'But why isn't she here?'

'We're only settling the details here. Which don't concern her. We're doing the cool planning. Being a woman, she would only get that in a muddle.'

I closed my eyes, and I saw the scene. In all its details. Heard Polyxena's laughter. Saw the murder in the temple – Achilles as a corpse, oh! who would not yearn to see that sight! – still clinging to Polyxena.

'You are using her.'

'Using whom?'

'Polyxena.'

'But aren't you capable of getting the point? It's not she we're concerned with. We're concerned with Achilles.'

'That's exactly what I'm saying.'

Until then my father had been silent. Now he spoke: 'Be silent, Cassandra!' Furiously, angrily. I said: 'Father— ' 'Don't try that on me any more,' he said. '"Father" – I indulged you for far too long.' 'All right,' I said, 'she's sensitive. All right, she does not see the world as it is. She's a bit up in the clouds. Takes herself seriously, women like to do that. She's spoiled, she can't fit in. High-strung. Stuck up.' 'About what, Daughter? Can you tell me that? With your nose always up in the air? And shooting off your mouth? And despising those who fight for Troy? After all, you know our situation. And if you don't endorse this plan of ours for killing Achilles, the worst of our enemies, right now – do you know what I'd call that? Lending aid and comfort to the enemy!'

Such stillness around me, inside me. Like now. Like here.

My father went on to say that not only should I

immediately endorse the plans which were up for deliberation; I should also undertake to keep silent about them and, once they were carried out, to expressly defend them against all comers.

So this, though unexpected, was the moment I had feared. I was not unprepared, why was it so hard? Rapidly, with uncanny rapidity I considered the possibility that they might be right. What does that mean, 'right'? Considered the possibility that the question of rights – Polyxena's right, my right – did not even arise because a duty, the duty to kill our worst enemy, ate up the right. And Polyxena? She was headed for ruin, no doubt about that. She was already a hopeless case.

'Now, Cassandra. You're going to be sensible, aren't you?'

I said: 'No.'

'You don't agree to the plan?'

'No.'

'But you will keep silent?'

'No,' I said. My mother Hecuba grasped my arm fearfully. She knew what was coming now; so did I. The king said: 'Seize her!'

Once again the hands grabbing me, not too hard, just enough to lead me away. Men's hands. No release through faints or visions. As we left I turned around; my look fell on my brother Paris. He did not want the blame, but what could he do? Did they not have him in their power for ever because of his blunder with

Helen? Weak, Brother, weak. A weakling. Hungry to conform. Just look at yourself in the mirror. With this final look I saw through him completely, and he saw through himself too, but he could not take it. More rashly than anyone he pressed on with that act of madness that was now inevitable. They say that afterward he let them display him, riding astraddle, to the people and the troops, as the conqueror of Achilles. 'Paris, our hero!' That could not diminish his self-contempt, which was incurable.

In profoundest darkness and uttermost stillness they led me to a place which I had always regarded as uncanny and menacing: the grave of the heroes. That is what we used to call it, and we children used it for our tests of courage. It lay apart, in a protruding and abandoned section of the fortress that gave directly onto the wall. Often (my hearing had grown un-believably acute) I could hear the sentries on patrol. They did not know that I was down there below them. No one knew except the two confidants of Eumelos who had taken me there (yes, Andron was with them, handsome Andron), and the two dissolute women who used to bring me food. I had never seen the like of those two in Troy before. Someone must have dug them up especially for me from the lowest depths, from the place people sink to when they have given up on themselves. They are intended to harshen my punishment, I thought at first; and I even caught myself thinking nonsensically, If only my father knew about that. Until the voice of reason asked me ironically: 'What if he did? Would they let me out of here? Would they bring me different women? Better food?'

No.

From the first hour on, I worked away incessantly at the wickerwork that lined the round cavity, where I could just barely stand up at the centre. I found a thin, loose strand of wicker (just as I found one now) and pulled it out of the weave – oh, it took hours, maybe days. I set out to release it completely, the whole length, as far as it went. For more than an hour now I have tried to do the same thing, but the willow basket where I am sitting is newer, its weave is not so rotted and filthy. I was seized, am seized, with zeal for the task, as if my life depended on it. At first – when to my good fortune I still felt numb and insensible and told myself they could not do this to me, not to me, not my father – I believed that they had buried me alive. For I did not know where I was, and I had heard them carefully wall up the hole after they put me in through it. The stench that assailed me. Such things did not exist. Where was I? How long does it take a person to starve to death? I crept around in the dust – what do I mean, dust, it was loathsome rot. Was my container round? Yes, round and lined with wicker, which did not admit a single ray of light even when a day and a night and another day had presumably gone by; so very likely it was thickly plastered with mud on the outside. That is what I thought, and I was right. Finally I found bones and realised where I was. Someone was moaning, 'Mustn't lose my mind, not now' – my voice.

I did not lose my mind.

Then after a long time the scraping sound. The trapdoor that opened close to the ground, I did not see anything! But with difficulty I found it out. The bowl was shoved in and I tipped it over when I reached for it – tipped over the water! Then the flat barley cake. And for the first time the lewd screeching of one of the women.

That was the underworld. But I had not been buried. I was not to die of hunger. Was I disappointed?

I could always refuse the food.

It would have been easy. It may be that that is what they expected. After two or three days, I believe, I began to eat. And during the long intervals – I hardly slept at all – I pulled, tugged, twisted, and tore at the wicker. Something that was stronger than everything else was tearing at me. Many days I thought of only one thing: one day it must be over.

What must be over?

I remember that suddenly I paused, sat for a long time without moving, struck by the lightning realisation: this is pain.

It was pain, which I had thought I knew. Now I saw that until then it had barely grazed me. You do not distinguish the boulder that buries you beneath it, but only the force of the impact; so my pain at the loss of everything I had called 'father' was threatening to crush me with its weight. The fact that I was able to give a name to the pain, the fact that it answered to its name, gave me a breath of air. One day it must be over. Nothing lasts for ever. This was the second breath of relief, although relief is too strong a word for it. There is a kind of pain that stops hurting because it is everything. Air. Earth. Water. Each bite of food. Each breath you draw, every movement. No, it is indescribable. I never spoke about it. No one asked me about it.

The wicker wand. Now I have gotten it free. Now I have it in my hand. Now it will not be much longer. I am hiding it. No one will find it. The tree it was cut from grew on the Scamander River. When the pain let me go, I began to talk. With the mice, whom I fed. With a snake, who lived in a cavity and twisted herself around my neck when I was sleeping. Then with the ray of light that penetrated the opening where the wicker wand had been removed. The dot of light gave me back the day. Then I talked to the women, something they had never experienced before. They were the scum of Troy; whereas I, immeasurably privileged, had wandered in the palace above them. Their vulgar glee at my plight was understandable. I noticed that they could not succeed in insulting me. They noticed it, too. Oh, the words they taught me. They spat at me from the shaft through which they crawled on their bellies to poke my food in through the trapdoor; the longer I was kept prisoner, the more greedily I waited for it. I did not know whether they understood what I said. I asked them their names. Shrill laughter. I told them mine. Contemptuous screeches. One of them (the younger judging by her voice) used to spit into my water bowl. I was forced to learn that not everyone can retrace his steps once he has been degraded to the level of an animal. The women turned more threatening. I began to be afraid of them.

One day the trapdoor scraped open when it was not mealtime. I waited in vain to hear a screech. A cultivated male voice – so such a thing did exist! – spoke to me. Andron. The handsome Andron. 'Here, Cassandra.' As if we were meeting at supper in the palace. 'Come here. Take this.' What was he giving me? Something hard, sharp. I felt it with trembling fingers. Did I recognise it? Oh, that beautiful voice, swollen with triumph. Yes – it was the sword-belt of Achilles. Which, as I must surely be able to imagine (he said), could have been obtained only by killing its wearer. Yes, everything had gone according to plan. Yes, the Greek hero Achilles was dead.

'And Polyxena? Please! Polyxena?'

Curtly, far too curtly: 'She's alive.'

The trapdoor fell, I was left alone. Now came the hardest part.

Achilles the brute was dead. The plot had been successful. If things had gone according to my wishes, the brute would still be alive. They had proved right. When you are successful, it proves you are right. But hadn't I known from the outset that I was not in the right? So. So had I gotten myself locked up because I was too proud to give in to them?

Well, I had time. I could re-examine the case, word by word, step by step, thought by thought. Ten times, a hundred times I stood before Priam, a hundred times I tried to agree with him, to answer yes at his command. A hundred times I said no again. My life, my voice, my body would produce no other answer. 'You don't agree?' No. 'But you will keep silent?' No. No. No. No.

They were right, and it was my portion to say no.

At last, at last the voices grew silent. One day I wept with happiness inside my basket. The younger of the two women pushed something in to me on top of the flat barley cake. My fingers recognised it at once even before my head could form the name: Anchises! Wood! One of his animals. A sheep? A lamb? Once I was outside I saw: it was a pony. Myrine sent it. She persuaded the younger of the warder women, I do not know how. Moreover, the woman stopped barking at me after that. Oh, I was so moved by that little piece of wood that I forgot to eat. They knew where I was. They had not forgotten me. I would live and be with them. We would not lose each other again until the inevitable happened, the fall of Troy.

And in fact that is how it happened. When I got out

I lived for a long time with my hands held in front of my eyes because I could not tolerate any light; and preferably inside the caves. Myrine, who did not leave my side, forced me little by little to look into the light. We did not talk about Penthesilea, or about her own wounds, until the last time we were together. I saw her naked. She was covered with scars. My skin was smooth until the end, until now. I hope they know their handiwork; then one cut will be enough. At that time only a woman could touch me. Aeneas came, he sat beside me, he stroked the air above my head. I loved him more than my life. He did not live with us like many young men whom the war had damaged in body or soul. They arrived like shadows; our blazing life restored their colour, blood, zest. When I close my eyes I see the picture. Mount Ida in the shifting light. The slopes with their caves. The Scamander, its banks. That was our world, no landscape could be more beautiful. The seasons. The scent of the trees. And our free existence, a new joy for each new day. The citadel did not reach as far as here. They could not fight the enemy and us at the same time. They left us alone, took from us the fruits we harvested, the cloth we wove. We ourselves lived in poverty. I remember that we sang a lot. Talked a lot, evenings by the fire in Arisbe's cave, where the figure of the goddess on the wall seemed to be alive. Killa and other women used to pray to her and place offerings. No one tried to stop them. We knew we were lost, but we did not force that knowledge on those who needed a firm hope. Our good cheer was not forced, though it never lost its dark undercoat. We did not stop learning. Each shared his own special knowledge with the other. I learned to make pots, clay vessels. I invented a pattern to paint on them, black and red. We used to tell each other our dreams; many of us were amazed at how much they revealed about us. But more than anything else we talked about those who would come after us. What they would be like. Whether they would still know who we were. Whether they would repair our omissions, rectify our mistakes. We racked our brains trying to think of a way we could leave them a message, but did not know any script to write in. We etched animals, people, ourselves inside the rock caves, which we sealed off before the Greeks came. We pressed our hands side by side into the soft clay. We called that immortalising our memory, and laughed. This turned into a touch-fest, where we spontaneously touched each other and got acquainted. We were fragile. Our time was limited and so we could not waste it on matters of minor importance. So we concentrated on what mattered most: ourselves – playfully, as if we had all the time in the world. Two summers and two winters.

In the first winter Hecuba (who sometimes came and sat with us quietly) sent Polyxena to us. She had lost her mind. She had gone crazy with fear. We found out that she could only bear to have soft things around her, gentle touches, dim light, muted sounds. We learned that as Achilles was dying in the temple, he had made Odysseus promise to sacrifice Polyxena, who had betrayed him, on his grave after the Greek victory. Her face was ravaged, but when she heard a flute playing far away, she was able to smile.

In the first spring Priam sent for me. I arrived and saw that no one recognised me in the streets of Troy. That was fine with me. My father, who did not say a word about anything that had happened, informed me dryly that we had a potential new ally, what was his name? Eurypylos. With fresh troops, not some-thing to be sneezed at. But he wanted me for his wife if he was to fight on our side.

We were silent for a while; then the king wanted to know my reply. I said: 'Why ever not?' My father wept feebly. I would have preferred him to be angry. Eurypylos arrived; there were worse men than he. He was killed the day after his first night with me, in one of the makeshift fights waged by the Greeks because they were unable to take the city. I went back to the Scamander again; no one mentioned my brief time away. During the last year of the war there was hardly one pregnant woman in Troy. Many looked enviously, compassionately, sadly at my belly. When the twins were born – it was hard, I lay in Arisbe's cave, once I cried out to the goddess: 'Cybele, help!' – they had many mothers. And Aeneas was their father.

I have experienced everything a person must experience.

Marpessa is laying both her hands against my back. Yes, I know. They will be coming soon. I would like to see that light once more. The light I used to watch together with Aeneas whenever we could. The light of the hour before the sun goes down. When every object begins to glow with its own light and gives off its own particular colour. Aeneas said: 'It wants to make a stand once more before the night.' I said: 'It wants to let the rest of its light and warmth stream out and then to let in the darkness and cold.' We could not help laughing when we realised that we were speaking in metaphors. That was how we lived in the hour before dark. The war, a wounded dragon incapable of further movement, lay heavy and faint over our city. The next move it made was bound to dash us to pieces. Abruptly, from one moment to the next, our sun could set. Lovingly and exactingly we followed its course on each of our days, for they were numbered. It amazed me to see that different though we all were, the women by the Scamander felt without exception that we were testing something, and that it was not a question of how much time we had. Nor of whether we could convince the majority of Trojans, who of course remained in the dismal city. We did not see ourselves as an example. We were grateful that we were the ones granted the highest privilege there is: to slip a narrow strip of future into the grim present, which occupies all of time. Anchises, who never tired of maintaining that it was always possible to do this; who was growing visibly weaker, was no longer able to go on weaving his baskets, and often had to lie down, but went on teaching that the spirit is higher than the body; who continued to fight with Arisbe (he used to call her the Great Mother, she had grown even bulkier, was lame in the hip, bridged with her trumpet of a voice distances she could no longer walk): Anchises, I believe, loved our life in the caves wholeheartedly, loved it without reservation, sadness, and scruple. He was fulfilling a dream of his and was teaching us younger ones how to dream with both feet on the ground.

Then it was over. One noon I woke up under the cypress tree where I often spent the hot hours of the day, and thought: 'Desolate. How desolate everything is.' The word came back again and again, each time ripping open the pit inside me.

Then a messenger came to Oenone: Paris was wounded. He was asking for her. Wanted her to save him. We watched her preparing the basket of herbs, bandages, and tinctures. Bending over: her beautiful white neck, which could hardly support the weight of the head any more. Paris had gotten rid of her at the time he needed the many girls. Grief for the man had eaten its way inside her, grief not on her account but on his. She could not get over the way he had changed. Like nature she remained identical in change. When she returned she was a stranger. Paris was dead. The temple physicians had summoned her too late. He had died in agony, of gangrene. Another woman hit with that same frozen look, I thought. As Paris's sister, I was supposed to attend his funeral. I did so. I wanted to see Troy again and found a grave. The inhabitants were all gravediggers who lived on only to bury themselves with sombre pomp in each of the dead. The rules of interment, which the priests continually elaborated and which had to be scrupulously observed, consumed the working day. Ghosts were carrying a ghost to the grave. I had never seen anything more unreal. And most ghastly of all was the figure of the king at the head of the procession, his decayed body draped in purple, being carried by four strong young men.

It was over. That evening on the wall I had the conversation with Aeneas after which we parted. Myrine never left my side again. Surely it was an illusion that the light over Troy seemed pale in the last days. Pale the faces. Vague the words we said.

We were waiting.

The collapse came swiftly. The end of the war was worthy of its beginning, an infamous deception. And my Trojan people believed what they saw, not what they knew. Believed that the Greeks would withdraw! And that they had left standing outside the wall this monster, which all the priests of Athena (to whom the thing was supposedly dedicated) rashly dared to call a 'horse.' So the thing was a 'horse.' Why so enormous? Who knows? As enormous as the reverence of our beaten foes for Pallas Athena, protectress of our city.

'Fetch the horse inside!'

That was going too far; I could not believe my ears. First I tried a matter-of-fact approach: 'Don't you see the horse is far too big for any of our gates?'

'Then we'll enlarge the wall.'

Now we paid the penalty for the fact that they hardly knew who I was any more. The shudder that had once attached to my name had already faded. The Greeks restored it to me. The Trojans laughed at my screeches. 'She's crazy, that one. Come on, break open the wall! Now bring in the horse!' Their anxiety to install this token of victory in their midst surpassed every other urge in intensity. Never were there victors like these, who in a mad frenzy transported the idol into the city. I feared the worst, not because I could see through the Greeks' plan move by move, but because I saw the baseless arrogance of the Trojans. I shrieked, pleaded, adjured, and spoke in tongues. I did not get to see my father, who, I was told, was unwell.

Eumelos. I was standing before him once again. I saw the face which you forget from time to time and which for that reason is permanent. Expressionless. Pitiless. Unteachable. Even if he believed me, he would not oppose the Trojans, and maybe get himself killed. He, for one, intended to survive (he said). And the Greeks would be able to use him. Wherever we came, he would be there first. And would pass us off with a shrug.

Now I understood what the god had ordained: 'You will speak the truth, but no one will believe you.' Here stood the No One who had to believe me; but he could not because he believed nothing. A No One incapable of belief.

I cursed the god Apollo.

The Greeks will tell their own version of what happened that night. Myrine was the first. Then blow after blow and cut after cut and thrust after thrust. Blood flowed through our streets, and the wail Troy uttered dug into my ears; since then I have heard it night and day. Now I will be freed from it. Later, fearing the images of the gods, they asked me if it was true that Ajax the Lesser had raped me by the statue of Athena. I said nothing. It was not beside the goddess. It was in the grave of the heroes, where we were trying to hide Polyxena while she screamed and sang. Hecuba and I stopped up her mouth with tow. The Greeks were searching for her in the name of their greatest hero, Achilles the brute. And they found her because her boyfriend, handsome Andron, betrayed her. Against his will (he bellowed), but what was he supposed to do, after all, they were threatening to kill him? Ajax the Lesser ran him through, laughing loudly. All of a sudden Polyxena was completely in her right mind. 'Kill me, Sister,' she begged softly. Oh, wretched woman that I was. I had arrogantly thrown away the dagger Aeneas had forced me to take at the end. I needed it not for myself but for my sister. When they dragged her away, Ajax the Lesser was on top of me. And Hecuba, as they held her fast, uttered curses whose like I had never heard before. 'A bitch,' Ajax the Lesser yelled when he was through with me. 'The Queen of the Trojans is a howling bitch.'

Yes. That is how it was.

And now the light is coming.

When I stood on the wall with Aeneas to watch the light for the last time, we quarrelled. Until now I have avoided thinking about it. Aeneas, who never badgered me, always let me be, did not want to twist or change anything about me, insisted that I go with him. He tried to order me. It was senseless to throw oneself into inevitable destruction, he said. I should take our children – he said that: *our* children! – and leave the city. A band of Trojans were prepared to do so, and they were not the worst people, either. They had taken on provisions and armed themselves, and were determined to fight their way through. To found a new Troy somewhere else. Begin again from the beginning. I deserved credit for my devotion. But enough was enough.

'You misunderstand me,' I said hesitantly. 'It's not for Troy's sake that I must stay, Troy does not need me. But for our sake. For your sake and mine.'

Aeneas. Dear one. You understood long before you

would admit it. It was obvious: the new masters would dictate their law to all the survivors. The earth was not large enough to escape them. You, Aeneas, had no choice: you had to snatch a couple of hundred people from death. You were their leader. 'Soon, very soon, you will have to become a hero.'

'Yes!' you cried. 'And so?' I saw by your eyes that you had understood me. I cannot love a hero. I do not want to see you being transformed into a statue.

Dear one. You did not say that it would not happen to you. Or that I could protect you from it. You knew as well as I did that we have no chance against a time that needs heroes. You threw the snake ring into the sea. You would have to go far, far away, and you would not know what lies ahead.

I am staying behind.

The pain will remind us of each other. When we meet later, if there is a later, we will recognise each other by it.

The light went out. Is going out.

They are coming.

Here is the place. These stone lions looked at her.

They seem to move in the shifting light.